Feuding . . .

Athena gasped. "Sex! You think I came to *seduce* you?"

"I think you came prepared to do whatever it takes to get back Kildrurry."

She was staring at him incredulously. "Including luring you to bed."

He leaned back in his chair. "If all else failed."

For a moment Athena was too shocked to protest. Then fury overcame disbelief. "Why you—you animal! How dare you?"

He eyed her coolly. "It's late, Athena. Surely you're not going to waste my time and yours by denying you came to Scotland to reclaim Kildrurry."

"I'm not going to deny a thing," she spat. "An accusation like that doesn't deserve a denial. It's too ludicrous. Everything my father said about the Burkes was right. It may be three hundred years, but some things just don't change. You're still a bunch of overbearing, arrogant, self-centered mercenaries!"

Dear Reader,

Welcome to Silhouette! Our goal is to give you hours of unbeatable reading pleasure, and we hope you'll enjoy each month's six new Silhouette Desires. These sensual, provocative love stories are both believable and compelling—sometimes they're poignant, sometimes humorous, but always enjoyable.

Indulge yourself. Experience all the passion and excitement of falling in love along with our heroine as she meets the irresistible man of her dreams and together they overcome all obstacles in the path to a happy ending.

If this is your first Desire, I hope it'll be the first of many. If you're already a Silhouette Desire reader, thanks for your support! Look for some of your favorite authors in the coming months: Stephanie James, Diana Palmer, Dixie Browning, Ann Major and Doreen Owens Malek, to name just a few.

Happy reading!

Isabel Swift
Senior Editor

SDRL-7/85

ERIN ROSS
Willing Spirit

Silhouette Desire

Published by Silhouette Books New York

America's Publisher of Contemporary Romance

SILHOUETTE BOOKS
300 East 42nd St., New York, N.Y.   10017

ISBN: 0-373-05280-4

First Silhouette Books printing May 1986

America's Publisher of Contemporary Romance

Printed in the U.S.A.

Books by Erin Ross

ERIN ROSS

has pursued a wide variety of activities during her life. At one time or another, this author studied radio, taught guitar, practiced karate and sang with a rock group. But writing has always been a favorite pursuit. "I'm an avid reader," she explains, "and I think sooner or later all avid readers get the bug to write!"

To my son, Christopher.

One

Straight ahead is the forebuilding—the part that juts out from the main body of the keep."

Athena MacKay followed the direction of the guide's arm toward the crumbling stone annex that protected the main entrance into the castle. Behind it, Kildrurry rose proud and massive despite long centuries of neglect.

That's all that's left of it, she thought, staring silently at the thirteenth-century keep. There's the MacKay heritage. Not much, is it? She raised a hand to shield the early-April sun from her eyes and studied the broken lines, the abrupt angles and pitted surface of the structure. What would Dad say if he could see it? she wondered. Would he still want me to fight for it?

The guide's voice broke into her musings. "Watch your step, ladies and gentlemen. The going can be treacherous here."

Silently Athena followed the handful of tourists toward the castle. Beneath a clear Scottish sky, the hillside angled raggedly upward, making the climb to the old keep every bit as precarious as their guide had warned. Carefully Athena avoided the occasional patch of snow and ice that lay hidden behind protective outcrops of rock, a chilly reminder that despite the show of sunshine, winter had not yet relinquished its claim on the rugged border countryside.

She was last to enter the old annex, and she stood well behind the group, still marveling that this pile of broken stones and weeds had so obsessed her father. What was it that has fascinated him about this place? Why had he been so driven to get it back?

Athena sighed and ran her hand along the rough surface of the wall, frowning at the initials irreverently carved into the stone. Kildrurry wasn't even very important as a fourteenth-century tourist attraction, she thought, remembering how difficult it had been to find a bus group that stopped here. Looking again at the crumbling walls, she felt a deep sadness. Was it worth it, Dad? she asked silently. Was Kildrurry really worth all the pain and frustration it caused you?

The profound heaviness that had settled upon Athena since entering Kildrurry grew more pronounced as the group passed through the annex and up a spiral stairway to the main body of the castle. Here the deterioration, although not as severe, was still extensive. Who would pay the bill for that? she wondered, estimating that the cost would far exceed Clan MacKay's modest savings. Even if I could work a miracle and get it back, how in the world could we afford it?

It was as they passed into the main hall of the castle that Athena's vague depression suddenly changed into something more disturbing. The moment she entered the large empty chamber she felt it. At first there was just a faint prickle at the base of her neck, bothersome, but not so uncommon as to be frightening. She'd had the feeling before, especially when she visited older houses or places where some violence had occurred. She would just ride it out. There was no cause for alarm.

But it wasn't the same. This time the sensation did not gently fade away. It moved down her spine like a series of small electric shocks. Trying to catch her breath, Athena leaned against the wall for support. She closed her eyes and fought to relax, struggling for deep, even breaths.

"You'll feel it, Athena." Her father's words came to her through a frightening whirlwind of emotions. "Go to Kildrurry. Go there and you'll understand!"

Deliberately Athena tried to clear her mind of all thoughts, even those of her father. Relax and flow with it, she repeated silently. Relax. Don't let it take you over.

Gradually her mind cleared; her pulse slowed and her breathing became less forced. As Athena's fear subsided, the energy around her seemed to take on substance. She felt surrounded by people she couldn't see but could feel—profoundly, intimately.

At some intuitive level of her consciousness, Athena knew that these people, these vague, shapeless forms, were her ancestors, all the MacKays who had gone before her. She felt a deep bond with them—as if she'd known them all her life. They were real; Kildrurry was real. These people, her kin, had spent most of their lives here. They'd loved and laughed, given birth and died within these rooms. Now, in a way she couldn't understand, they seemed to be reaching out to her.

"If you'll follow me—"

Athena was so lost in the past that the guide's voice came as a shock. For several moments she continued to lean against the rough stones, too weak to move. Her hands felt cold and clammy; her body was bathed in a fine sheen of perspiration.

"Miss. Miss, are you all right?"

Looking up, Athena saw that the tour group had left the room. The guide was regarding her with alarm.

"Yes, I'm fine, thank you," Athena told the woman a bit shakily. "I just felt a little dizzy. I'm all right now."

As if in a dream, Athena followed the group through the remainder of the castle. The tour droned on, but she was oblivious to the historical dates, the occasional points of interest, the medieval architecture. Her senses were overwhelmed by what she had experienced. Athena walked in a daze, the ghosts of the past now far more real to her than the flesh-and-blood people of the present.

She hadn't expected anything like this. Athena had come to Scotland because it had been her father's last wish and because she was the most logical, perhaps the *only* MacKay with a chance of reclaiming Kildrurry. As a daughter, it was a final gift to a beloved parent. As a scientist, the trip was an intriguing opportunity to study a phenomenon that had fascinated her since childhood. She'd come prepared to investigate the MacKays, to try, if possible, to set the record straight. What happened a few moments ago was much more than she had bargained for.

The group had come out onto the east rampart, or roof-walk, across the front of the castle. Grateful for the cool breeze that swept across the parapet, Athena hung behind the rest, breathing deeply to clear her head. The country-side that surrounded the castle had a primeval look to it. She thought it was probably much the same now as it had been for centuries. Standing here, Athena couldn't help wondering how many other MacKays had looked out on this same sight. How many dreams were woven here? she mused. And how many were dashed by the latest horde of invaders sweeping over hills?

As if he were part of her daydream, Athena caught sight of a giant of a man standing with several other men on what had once been the keep's main drawbridge, but which was now a permanent wooden structure spanning the dry, overgrown moat below. For a startled moment she had the irrational feeling that he'd walked straight out of the past. Athena blinked, then viewed the man more objectively. It was his size, she realized, that was responsible for the illusion. He was so tall and muscular, and his hair was such a bright, fiery gold, that he might well have been one of the medieval Norsemen of her imaginings.

Athena watched as the stranger turned his face toward the castle, then she quickly moved back a step as his eyes raised suddenly to the parapet. A few paces down the rampart, she saw the guide point down excitedly toward the men and realized it was the woman's voice that had drawn the man's attention. Breathlessly the guide explained the significance of the little group below them, obviously delighted that her tour had been enlivened by such unexpected fare.

The sound of the tall man's name turned Athena's blood to ice. Sir Christopher Burke! My God, it was actually him. The coincidence took her several moments to assimilate. She hadn't expected to find him here. Standing well behind the gunport opening, she surreptitiously watched him first look up at the tour group, then turn his attention back to his companions.

"Are they really going to tear down the castle to build a golf course?" A small woman with a Southern accent was looking down at the men with an expression of regret on her rather plain face. "It seems a shame. I mean, Kildrurry is so old. I thought England and Scotland were proud of their old castles."

"Kildrurry is privately owned," the guide explained. "For the past 350 years it's been part of the Burke-family estate." She motioned around them. "As you can see, the keep needs extensive work. Even the most basic renovations would require a sizable outlay of capital. And there's little guarantee of a return. Kildrurry is so far off the main tourist track . . ."

The guide let her words fade into the breeze as she smiled sweetly at her charges. Athena heated and tried to repress a feeling of intense dislike for the woman. It wasn't her fault that Sir Christopher was selling out the Mac-Kays. But now that she'd been here, just the thought of Kildrurry being torn down, and for a golf course of all things, made her blood boil. What right did Sir Christopher have to destroy what was left of the MacKay heritage? What right did any of the Burkes have to wield that kind of power?

The group on the drawbridge was gone when they returned to the outer ward. Briskly the guide herded the handful of tourists toward the minibus that all day had transported them round and about the border countryside. Strictly business now, the woman glanced meaningfully at her watch as if to remind her charges that the tour was, after all, bound by a finite time schedule.

As before, Athena took a seat at the rear of the vehicle, turning back to watch the massive stone walls recede in the distance. Without really absorbing the words, she heard the guide announce their final stop for the day. But for Athena the tour was over. She'd seen what she'd come for—and gotten much more than she'd expected!

She leaned her head back on the seat and let her mind drift free of the talk around her, attempting to make some sense of her unexpected reaction to Kildrurry. The scientist in Athena needed to sort it out. Why had she been so affected by an ancient pile of stones lying in the midst of a barren Scottish countryside? What was it about the old castle that had touched her so profoundly?

The answer evaded logical reasoning. Of course she'd been influenced by her father's dying wish, but that alone couldn't account for the unusual depth of the experience. Kildrurry had touched her in a way that went beyond filial devotion, however strong. She couldn't explain it; it made no rational sense. Yet as she caught her last glimpse of the castle, perched alone and proud on the hill, her father's words echoed again in her ears. "You'll understand when you see it, Athena. You'll know then why you must save Kildrurry!"

Athena checked out of her hotel the following afternoon, then drove her rented car east out of Edinburgh toward the North Sea coastline. Once off the main highway, she followed the map along narrow, winding roads toward North Berwick. Somewhere ahead lay Burke House. She felt a sense of fear mingled with anticipation. Since her visit to Kildrurry the day before, the trip to Burke House had taken on a new meaning. The old MacKay clan seat was no longer just a name in one of her father's stories. It was real; she'd seen it, felt it, intimately sensed its past.

And Christopher Burke was real, too. Involuntarily her fingers clenched the wheel a little tighter as she thought about the man she'd seen the day before on the drawbridge. Athena still couldn't shake a mental image of the golden-haired giant wearing armor and brandishing a Viking's sword. Over the course of an uneasy night, she'd decided the fantasy was provoked by more than his sheer size. He seemed to be fired by an inner power, a force of personality that was frankly intimidating. She'd been obliged to reassess her strategy. How would a man like that react if he discovered someone had entered his home under false pretenses? No matter how authentic her credentials, how long could she realistically expect to conceal the true purpose of her visit?

She was so lost in her thoughts that the first sight of Burke House took her by surprise. Athena stopped the car and stared at the thirteenth-century castle that loomed sharply at the top of the cliff. Again she felt prickles start at the base of her neck, less intense this time, but warning her nonetheless. Without bothering to analyze the feeling, she knew that Kildrurry and Burke House were integrally intertwined. For good or for evil, the Burkes and the MacKays were bound together in time.

Athena leaned forward in her seat and studied the old castle. Although in far better repair than Kildrurry, Burke House seemed just as much a fortress, imposing and stark, with few frills to relieve the uncompromising rock-gray exterior. From her father she knew that the original structure had been largely destroyed in the late sixteenth century by a marauding band of English, to be rebuilt, more or less in its present state, by a determined Burke ancestor. Four hundred years later, she had to admit, it was still an imposing sight. High on a cliff, its back turned to the sea, the place reeked of atmosphere. Watching it, she felt another sharp stab of apprehension; in real life it was so much more formidable than it had seemed in her father's stories!

"What have you gotten me into, Dad?" she muttered warily. "What in the name of all that's rational am I letting myself in for?"

Squaring her shoulders, she released the brake and coaxed the car up the remaining quarter mile of the climb. Pulling to a stop, Athena looked up at the house once more before stepping out onto the roughly paved road. As she did, a cold wind tore at her clothes. It was freezing, although the sun continued to shine determinedly in the cloudless sky. It should be storming, she thought, making her way to the top of the stairs. This place cries out for some good old-fashioned thunder and lightning.

Athena reached out for the intricately carved gargoyle knocker, the only visible device for announcing her arrival. She paused a fraction of a moment, then pounded it several times against the heavy oak door. The sound echoed like some eerie effect from an old horror movie.

"Very impressive," she told the gargoyle, eyeing the malicious grin. "Even without a storm you make a formidable welcoming committee." The creature's grotesque face leered back at her, seemingly unimpressed by either Athena or the compliment. "Let's just hope," she added beneath her breath, "that you aren't a forewarning of what I can expect inside."

The door opened suddenly, and considering its size and age, with a minimum amount of noise. Inside, an elderly manservant stood looking at her dourly. "Yes?" he asked brusquely.

"I'm Athena Ramsey," she told him, smiling nervously. Carefully she omitted her family name as she had in all her correspondence. "I believe Mrs. Burke is expecting me."

"Come in." The man's expression remained uninviting as she stepped across the threshold, and she could feel his frosty gaze on her back as he closed the door behind her. "Wait here," he added curtly, then turned to walk up a wide, curving stairway that led off of the entrance hall.

"That's abrupt enough," Athena murmured, watching the man disappear around the first landing. For a heart-stopping moment she'd been afraid her ruse had already been discovered. It's just your nerves, she told herself firmly. And you're not really a fraud—you've been on dozens of visits like this. It's just another case.

Taking a deep breath, Athena turned and gave her full attention to the room. Now that she was alone, she realized the full enormity of the place. One side of the high-ceilinged hallway was lined with a series of large old tapestries, the other was completely taken up by the stairway. Statuary and suits of armor vied with bagpipes and swords for her attention.

While she waited, Athena walked to the nearest tapestry and studied the soldiers who were depicted fighting in hand-to-hand combat. Despite the faded condition of the work, she recognized the famous battle at Bannockburn, the fourteen-century Scottish victory over the British.

"I don't want to like it but I do," she murmured as she continued her examination of the room. "Look at all this history, and the way it's been maintained." She felt a sudden resentment that Kildrurry had been allowed to fall into such disrepair. "How much was lost there, I wonder? How much that we'll never be able to reclaim?"

She was examining the suit of armor that guarded the dining room when the butler returned. He came up behind her so quietly that she jumped at the sound of his voice.

"Follow me."

Without waiting for a reply he turned and made his way back up the stairs. A man of few words, Athena thought as she silently followed the straight, thin figure. Would Clara Burke be equally unfriendly? she wondered. Athena thought back to her weeks of correspondence with Sir

Christopher's grandmother. For the most part, the old woman's letters had been straightforward, if not precisely friendly. But they *had* resulted in an invitation to Burke House. That was the main thing. Step number one, she reminded herself. *Get inside!*

The butler opened a door to the left of the first landing. Without a word he motioned for Athena to enter, then silently closed the door behind her. She allowed her eyes a moment or two to adjust to the dim light, then realized someone—an old woman—was sitting in a chair by the window. On closer inspection she realized it was a wheelchair.

"Come in. Come in." The woman squinted at her through rimless glasses. "Open these drapes, will you, lass, so I can have a better look at you."

Athena pulled open the heavy draperies, then turned back to the woman. Clara Burke was tiny, with snow-white hair and a lined, weathered face. Her hands, which moved nervously when she talked, were bony and darkened by protruding veins and age spots. She was wearing a dressing gown and slippers, and her long fine hair had been carefully drawn back from her face. Her voice was high, with the tendency to shrillness common in most slightly deaf persons; her faded blue eyes were alert and interested. Athena was momentarily taken aback by the woman's apparent infirmity. Clara Burke's letters had seemed so self-assured. She found them at odds with the frail old woman sitting in front of her now.

"Sit down, lass." Mrs. Burke nodded toward a straight chair, and Athena dutifully pulled it closer to the woman and took a seat. "You're younger than I thought you'd be," Clara went on, tilting her head a bit as she took Athena's measure. "And bonnie, too. Milton Bruce said you knew what you were about. But I had to satisfy myself that what he said was true."

Athena felt a pang of guilt. She knew all about the glowing recommendation Milton had given her. All part of the plan, she thought uncomfortably. But she was here, she told herself, remembering Kildrurry. And Milton had apparently felt no stirrings of conscience.

"I've had nearly five years experience, Mrs. Burke," she told the old woman seriously. "And I've read extensive historical literature about your, ah, problem."

"Och! Angus MacKay! The old bounder's a problem, no doubt about it. Been drivin' me fair out of my mind for longer than I care to remember." She leaned forward and eyed Athena sharply. "You do believe in ghosts then, lass?"

Athena had to smile. One way or another this was the question her clients invariably asked upon meeting her, some out of curiosity, most because they needed reassurance about their own sanity.

"I wouldn't be a psychic investigator if I didn't believe the world is full of things that can't be explained by our five senses," she told the old woman quietly. "I'm convinced something exists beyond that dimension."

Clara Burke sat back, squinting at the younger woman. "So what you're sayin' then, is that you've got an open mind."

"Yes, Mrs. Burke," Athena said, matching her sobriety. "I can promise you an open mind."

The woman clapped her hands together, her pale blue eyes sparkling. "Good! I judged from your letters we'd get on. And Milton's a shrewd man—I knew he'd not let me down." She rubbed her hands together eagerly. "We'll start tomorrow then."

Athena experienced a shiver of excitement. [The] she'd had on the road looking up at the castle [was] stronger now that she was inside. Her scientifi[c] was whetted. If only she had the time to complete her investigation. If only Christopher Burke didn't unmask her first!

"I'd love to start tomorrow, Mrs. Burke," Athena said cautiously. "But what about the rest of the household? I assume they know why I'm here?"

The woman clicked her tongue. "Gram, lass. Call me Gram."

"Gram," Athena repeated. "You see, it's important that everyone work together in a case like this."

"It's just me grandson, Christopher. He has no parents, poor lad. And sad to say, he's not a believer. For all that's happened, he closes his eyes and refuses to see what's at the end of his nose."

Athena felt a prickle of alarm. "But if he objects to my being here—"

"Och! Dinna fash yersel'. He'll not give you trouble. I'll see to that."

Athena looked at the frail old woman, unable to still her conscience. "I'd hate to cause any problems between you and your grandson." She glanced at Mrs. Burke's wheelchair and Gram laughed.

"Bide a wee, lass. For all his newfangled ways, Christopher knows full well how I feel about this business. He'll not go against me." She patted Athena's hand, then looked disdainfully at her wheelchair. "And don't be fooled by this wheely contraption. I may have seen my last of eighty, but there are a few more years left in this old body."

She leaned forward, this time grasping Athena's hand so tightly that the younger woman almost cried out. Gram's face had grown taut, and her blue eyes blazed dark with determination. "Nay, lass, I'm not yet ready to go to my grave. Not until I've rooted out that miserable scoundrel, Angus MacKay. And for that I need you. Promise me you won't leave Burke House until you've done this job. Promise me that!"

Athena could only look at her in stunned silence. The old woman's words were so similar to those spoken by her father just before his death ten months before that she found it difficult to speak.

"Promise me, lass," the woman persisted.

"I'll...I'll do my best," answered Athena haltingly. "I promise you that I'll do my very best."

The old woman looked at her shrewdly, then nodded. "Aye, I can see by your eyes that you will. More than that I cannot ask." She reached for a tasseled cord by her chair and gave it a sharp tug. "Lachlan will see you to your room. Dinner is at seven. I don't get downstairs as much as I used to, but Christopher will keep you company. I think you'll find him a good lad."

Athena thought about the old woman's words as she followed Lachlan's rigid back up yet another flight of stairs and down several confusing turns in the hall until they reached her room. She found it difficult to reconcile Gram's "good lad" with the strapping giant she'd seen yesterday at Kildrurry. She sensed that the man on the bridge was nobody's fool. She remembered the craggily handsome face, the cool, intelligent eyes, the firmly set mouth. If, as Gram said, he was not a believer, what would he think of Athena's presence in his home? More to the point, what would he do if he found out she was a MacKay?

"This is your room, miss. Your bags have been unpacked."

Athena stood amazed in the doorway of the room that had been allotted to her during her stay at Burke House. Once again she experienced that strange feeling of having stepped back in time. After Lachlan silently departed, she took stock of her temporary home.

The room was large and furnished with a canopied bed and several matching dark oak pieces. The ceiling was very high and coved all around, while the four corners were decorated with elaborate carvings. Even here, the walls were embellished with embroidered tapestries—lovely but not quite up to the quality of those she'd admired downstairs. Undoubtedly they'd been hung as much to keep out the drafts as for aesthetic reasons, she thought, rubbing her hands together briskly. Too bad they hadn't been more successful.

More than anything else, Athena decided, Burke House was cold. Despite the thickness of the walls, the outside chill seemed to permeate every corner of the castle. Lachlan had laid a fire in the small fireplace across from the bed, but it was sputtering fitfully and she doubted it would catch. She'd also been supplied with a small space heater as well, but eyeing the undersize appliance, she had little hope that it would be up to the task of heating the large room.

Walking over to the window, Athena pulled back the heavy draperies and stared out at the darkening afternoon and the ominous clouds that were forming to the east. She'd guessed from walking upstairs that her room faced the rear of the castle, but she was startled to see how close the sea actually was from her window. She sucked in her breath as increasing winds pounded the surf against the rocky cliffs below. Burke House fits here, she thought. It's like an extension of the hill—a part of it. Her mind turned toward the master of the castle. Christopher Burke fit, too, she mused. The medieval Norseman—the conqueror. And, unless she was very much mistaken, a formidable adversary!

Athena thought of her father and the trust he had put in her. The oldest of three children, Athena had been unusually close to MacKay. Security and stability, if not affluence, had always been present in her home, and the MacKays had been fairly representative of the typical midwestern family. At least externally.

Perhaps the most glaring difference between Athena's family and that of her friends was her father's preoccupation with his Scottish ancestry. Other children in Athena's neighborhood came from ethnic backgrounds. But for the most part, they had long since assimilated into the mainstream of American culture. One family simply didn't vary that much from its neighbors.

Athena's home was the exception. There, observance of Scottish tradition was faithfully, enthusiastically, followed. From her earliest childhood, Athena remembered her father playing his bagpipes and regaling his family with Scottish ditties and a seemingly inexhaustible store of folklore. As she grew older, this puzzled her. It wasn't as if her father had come from Scotland; the MacKays were fourth-generation Americans. But at some point during his formative years, John MacKay had discovered his roots, and from that moment on they had strongly influenced his life.

And those roots had brought her to Scotland. Athena wondered what her mother would think if she knew the real reason her daughter had come to North Berwick. Not sure what might come of the trip, Athena had decided to adopt a "wait and see" attitude before involving her mother. If Susan MacKay suspected Athena's motives, she'd had the tact, or the understanding, to keep her thoughts to herself. Just as she had ten years before when Athena first developed a driving interest in human behavior—and worse, at least to her friends—a fascination with *paranormal* behavior.

Through it all—her husband's obsession with his clan, her daughter's interest in the world of the occult—Susan MacKay had calmly gone about her own business, giving unconditional love to her husband and children and happily leaving them all to follow their own paths. A mother in a million, Athena thought fondly. Who else could have endured her father's eccentricities for more than thirty years? And so happily, at that!

Shaking herself out of her thoughts, Athena moved away from the window to sort through the oak cupboard for something to wear to dinner. "It's got to be warm," she murmured, rubbing her arms briskly. "That's the key word here, warmth."

She settled on a wool dress with long sleeves and knee-length suede boots. Laying her clothes out on the bed, she soaked in a tub of steaming water in an adjoining bathroom that looked as if it had been added in a fairly recent modernization of the castle. Despite her efforts to relax, however, her trepidation mounted with every passing moment.

"You're a coward, Athena MacKay," she told her reflection in the mirror, as she redid her hair for the dozenth time. "You've been in difficult situations before. And you've survived."

But you've never been up against someone like Christopher Burke, a little voice added. Sir Christopher isn't just another difficult job. He's a Burke. He's the enemy!

With a mutter of defeat, Athena gave up the attempt to sort out her curls and was simply giving her hair a good brushing when a young woman wearing a maid's uniform arrived to show her downstairs.

"I'm Fiona, miss," she informed Athena quietly as they walked down the corridor. The girl's voice was tiny, almost like a child's. In fact, she was hardly bigger than a young girl, with petite hands and feet and long, very dark hair pulled into a neat ponytail beneath her ruffled white cap. A loud boom of thunder punctuated their arrival at the stairs.

"There seems to be a storm coming," Athena said, attempting light conversation.

"Yes, miss. It's already rainin'. It will probably get worse durin' the night."

"I suppose you get a lot of storms here on the North Sea," Athena asked.

"Oh, yes, miss," the girl answered, a note of pride in her soft voice. "It's often we're stuck up here for days while they work on the roads."

"I see." Athena found the prospect grim. But surely the girl meant during the winter. It was now the first week in April. Even this far north the weather must acknowledge the onset of spring.

"Sir Christopher said to show you to the library," Fiona went on, breaking into Athena's thoughts. "He'll be down shortly."

With a little curtsy, the young woman left her charge at the entrance to a large rectangular room. Another chapter from Scottish history, Athena thought, walking inside to eye the dark, square furniture and heavy wine-colored drapes. The room was far bigger than Athena's notion of a home library, although admittedly much of the wall space was taken up by books. The far side of the chamber was dominated by a huge stone fireplace, and she was grateful to see an enormous fire blazing in its cavernous interior. In front of the hearth was a soft, oversize gray seal rug.

They don't do anything here in a small way, she thought, standing in front of the open grate. Athena rubbed her hands together as close to the heat as she dared, enjoying the warmth that spread deliciously through her body. Despite her resolve to remain calm, however, her natural confidence continued to wane as the moments passed, rhythmically ticked off by an ancient grandfather's clock in the corner. Athena found herself counting the strokes of the pendulum as she waited.

"This is ridiculous," she murmured, stepping away from the fire. "At this rate you'll be a bundle of nerves before he ever gets here."

Restlessly she circled the room, examining the books and trying to date the paintings scattered almost negligently between the stacks. After several minutes of this, her eye was caught by a large, very old volume set open on a stand opposite the clock. Walking over, she ran her hand over the embossed title. *Campbell's Chronicle of Scottish Clans.* Carefully turning the pages, she admired the intricate color illustrations, still vivid despite the book's age. Commencing with the fifteenth century, the book traced the growth of Scottish clans through the mid-1800s. Athena was captivated. It was a beautiful work.

She came to a frayed red velvet ribbon and saw that it marked a section detailing the Clan Burke. She studied the spiderlike script, then searched the book for her own family tartan. The page she sought fell open easily. Too easily. Athena wondered about this as she read the worn monograph that chronicled her ancestors. Some long-ago Burke must have spent a lot of time studying his MacKay rivals, she thought. Or could the interest be more recent?

Was the curious party someone currently living at Burke House?

"There are enough ghosts in there to keep you busy for a lifetime."

Athena whirled at the sound of his voice, then caught her breath at the sight of the man who seemed to fill the library door. In her surprise, her elbow knocked the book stand and she lurched around to stop it from toppling over. When she turned back, he was studying her with an unnerving calm.

"I'm sorry if I startled you, Miss Ramsey," he said quietly. "I'm Christopher Burke."

Two

Athena rarely found herself at a loss with someone. But to her intense dismay, this was one of those times. For an uncomfortable moment everything around her faded as the man in the doorway dominated her vision. Then he stepped forward into the room, and she experienced a stab of apprehension so intense that she had to stop herself from backing away. She was aware that her pulse had accelerated and when she tried to swallow her mouth was too dry.

"Are you interested in a particular clan?" He was looking beyond her at the book, still open she realized, to the MacKays. Trying to appear casual, she turned around and flipped back the pages.

"I was admiring the illustrations," she said, avoiding a direct lie. "It's a lovely book." Belatedly she held out her hand. "I'm happy to meet you, Sir Christopher."

The hand that returned her shake nearly dwarfed her own, and she had a feeling of repressed power in the grip. "And I'm curious to meet you, Miss Ramsey." His clear blue eyes were cool, almost glacial. He was so tall that Athena, who considered herself above average height at five-foot-eight, had to tilt her head back to look up at him. "I've never had the pleasure of meeting a ghost buster before."

"You've been seeing too many movies, Sir Christopher," she told him, keeping her tone pleasant despite his obvious sarcasm. "Actually, I'm a psychic investigator."

"I stand corrected," he said, giving her a mocking little nod. For a moment he'd been taken aback by her beauty, but had promptly put aside the distraction. Without a flicker of expression he reminded himself that it was not the external woman with whom he was concerned. "Psychic investigator. A very impressive title. And just what do you investigate, Miss Ramsey, if not ghosts?"

"I'm usually called in to study a phenomenon that falls outside the sphere of more conventional investigative channels," she answered smoothly. The usual questions, she thought. He was another doubting Thomas. Perhaps a bit more cynical than most, but nothing she hadn't handled before.

He raised an arrogant, faintly taunting eyebrow. "And just how do you appraise this *phenomenon*, may I ask?"

The mockery in his tone goaded her, yet she doggedly met his gibe with a smile only she knew was forced. "People have different preconceptions of how I work," she said, using the line that almost invariably put new clients at ease. "A woman in Georgia expected me to arrive with my turban and crystal ball. A local reporter wanted to know if I practiced any voodoo rites."

"And do you?"

For a moment she was taken aback. "Do I what?"

"Use a crystal ball, or any other gadgets for conjuring up your hobgoblins." Once again he saw a quick flash of temper cross her face. He approved of her control even as he pressed his advantage. "I'm afraid my knowledge in this area is a bit sketchy. I'm used to dealing with more—earthly pursuits. You'll have to educate me, Miss Ramsey."

This time the sarcasm in his voice was so blatant that she silently counted to ten before answering. "You'll be relieved to know that I'm fully accredited, Sir Christopher," she told him, keeping her voice matter-of-fact. "My undergraduate work is in psychology and I hold a master's degree in experimental psychology with an emphasis on the paranormal. While I work on my doctorate, I help feed myself by taking on private consultations similar to your grandmother's. For the past four and a half years, I've worked extensively with Dr. James Clausen of Duke University's parapsychology laboratory." She tilted her head up at him. "Anything else you'd care to know?"

Once again, the disdainful brow rose. "I *am* impressed. You seem more than adequately qualified for, ah, what you do. Although I must say I'm amazed to hear that it's possible to make a living in such an unorthodox profession."

"You'd be surprised how many people don't share your feelings on the subject," she managed with commendable understatement.

"Oh, really. I would have expected my point of view to be the rule rather than the exception." A faint hint of a smile played about his eyes, but it was of condescension rather than humor. "I've always thought that belief in the supernatural was something one outgrew with age and education."

"Or something one refuses to accept because of closed-minded prejudice!" The man was getting to her. Athena took a deep breath and lowered her voice. "You know it amazes me that psychic research constantly has to defend itself. It's even more fantastic when you stop to think that equally recent sciences, such as advanced electronics and space travel, have become perfectly respectable occupations."

"Do you honestly expect me to equate electronics and space travel with ghost hunting?"

"I told you, I'm a psychic investigator. I don't hunt ghosts!"

Christopher lifted his shoulder indifferently. "Oh? I was under the impression that was what brought you to Burke House. Correct me if I'm wrong, but my grandmother did inform you of our resident boogeyman."

"If you're referring to the manifestations she's been experiencing, yes, she did."

"Manifestations," he repeated doubtfully. "I don't think I'd go that far. Imagination, perhaps."

"Your grandmother doesn't strike me as being a particularly fanciful woman," she countered, annoyed that he could so casually dismiss the old woman's fears.

"My grandmother is eighty-three, Miss Ramsey. Neither her hearing, nor her eyesight are what they used to be. She's also very influenced by Scottish culture. And Scotland, more than most countries, has a rich tradition of *bogles* and *ghaisties*. It makes for interesting storytelling, but as a matter of practicality..." He left the words hanging.

"Ah, yes, good old practicality." She tilted her head to look at him. "And you're a very practical man, aren't you, Sir Christopher?" Oxford graduate, noted developer and entrepreneur, master of Burke House, she recited silently.

No, she thought, Christopher Burke would not believe in *bogles* and *ghaisties* and things that go bump in the night.

"I would make a very poor businessman if I weren't practical," he told her reasonably.

"Are you telling me you take everything at face value?"

"Everything?" Once again that derisive half smile played about his cool eyes and to her dismay, Athena found herself flushing at the intimate way he was studying her. "No, Miss Ramsey," he went on, fully aware of her discomfort. "I wouldn't say I take *everything* at face value."

He punctuated his words with a slow, very deliberate assessment of her from the tip of her curly head to the toes of her boots. His eyes took in the smooth, oval-shaped face, the generous mouth, the small straight nose, the flashing hazel eyes, the determined chin. He noted that the bones in her face displayed character rather than elegance. She was tall and narrow waisted, her figure slender if fully curved. Her clothes were sensible, but showed a certain flair in color and style. He saw her flush an even deeper red at his inspection, but it wasn't until she looked thoroughly disconcerted that he finally turned and walked to a bar set up on the sideboard. "Will you join me in a drink?"

"No, thank you," she replied shortly, furious at his arrogance.

Again, his look was faintly mocking. "Not even a wee dram," he persisted. "It's a cold night."

Athena started to refuse again, then decided she would never get anywhere unless she maintained her control. He might be infuriating, but she was a guest in his house. To that extent, at least, she would have to play by his rules. "All right," she said, with as much civility as she could muster. "But just a small one."

Moving back to the fireplace, she watched him as he
mixed the drinks. Despite his brief lapse into Gaelic, Athena was surprised that Christopher Burke's voice sounded
more of London than North Berwick. She could detect
only the slightest burr of *r*'s in the deep, resonant tones, to
proclaim his Scottish heritage. It must be his English
schooling, she decided. The Oxford-educated medieval
warrior. Now there was a combination!

She studied him more closely. If she'd been in awe of
Christopher Burke the previous day at Kildrurry, standing in the same room with him was nearly overwhelming.
Broad shouldered and muscularly lean, he really did have
the look of a warrior. His cheekbones were high, his nose
long and slightly crooked at the bridge as if it had once
been broken, his mouth lined with a cynicism that looked
as if it never took anything for granted. Full, sandy-
colored eyebrows swept to either side of his slate-blue eyes,
adding to the untamed look of his face.

Although he had all the ingredients to be termed handsome, it was not a word that would adequately describe
him. His face was too hard for that, as if he'd lost the en-
thusiasm of youth. Athena decided he had the look of a
man who'd experienced life and found it harsh and uncompromising. And like a wolf who must adapt to survive, he had become harsh and uncompromising, as well.

Suddenly his eyes came up to meet hers, and she thought
she knew how the early Scots must have felt in the face of
a Viking invasion. "And what is your verdict, Miss Ramsey?" he asked, walking over to hand her one of the
glasses.

Caught in the act of staring, Athena stammered, "I—I
beg your pardon?"

"I wondered what you saw—just now when you were
evaluating me. You claim to be an investigator, Miss

Ramsey. Well, what did you detect?'' Carrying his own drink, he went to stand at the opposite side of the hearth where he continued to regard her with amused curiosity.

Athena wished he had chosen somewhere else to stand. With a man of Christopher Burke's size, even a distance of four or five feet seemed far too intimidating.

"Well?" he pressed.

Perhaps it was his relentless goading that set her off, but Athena impulsively decided to be direct. "I see a skeptic, Sir Christopher. I see a man who believes in little besides himself. You strike me as a person who knows what he wants and doesn't hesitate to go after it. Financially, you're a winner, but I'm not sure you've learned the art of losing." When he didn't stop her, she swirled her drink thoughtfully and continued to appraise him.

"You have good taste, a well-developed sense of history and the money to indulge them both," she went on, thinking of what she had seen so far in Burke House. "My guess is that you have little patience for those who don't share your views, or those whom you consider to be 'losers.' You're a determined man, Sir Christopher, and I suspect that beneath that inflexible reserve, there's one hell of a temper waiting to explode at anyone foolish enough to cross you.

"If you can't see something, taste it, hold it, smell it or hear it, it simply doesn't exist. For some reason, I sense you're not very trusting and that you don't easily share your feelings."

Pleased with her assessment, she smiled at him from across the fireplace. "Well? How close was I?"

His expression remained noncommittal. "A few hits. A few misses."

"That's not fair. You have to be more explicit."

The cynical lines at the edge of his hard mouth tightened. "I don't share my feelings easily, remember?" He watched her as he sipped his drink. "You have a lively imagination, Miss Ramsey. But then I suppose that goes with your profession."

It was her turn to look at him coolly. "You keep harking back to that. Considering your feelings on the subject, I'm frankly surprised you allowed me into Burke House at all."

"Curiosity, perhaps."

Once again Athena's temper got the better of her. He made her feel like an insect under a microscope. "If you'd prefer I didn't stay, just say so and I'll leave."

The minute the words were spoken, Athena regretted them. She'd known the man less than half an hour and already she was allowing him to bait her. In frustration, she took a long sip of her drink, then caught her breath as the fiery liquid burned down her throat. "Is that—what you consider a—wee dram?" she managed.

"It's very fine, very old vintage Scotch, Miss Ramsey. And as such, it should be sipped, not gulped." He eyed her speculatively. "I take it you're not much of a drinker."

"You can take it that I'm not used to downing straight whisky." She walked over to the bar, chose a bottle of soda and sprayed in enough of the bubbly liquid to turn the Scotch a very pale amber. Despite the chill in the room, she avoided going back to the fireplace. Putting some distance between the two of them would not be a bad idea, she decided.

Looking back at him, she realized he'd correctly interpreted the maneuver. He was entirely too discerning, she thought in annoyance. She'd have to be careful.

"What *do* you do?" he asked, breaking the awkward silence.

When she looked confused, he clarified, "We've established that you don't go in for crystal balls—and you aren't wearing a turban, at least not tonight. How do you go about conducting one of your investigations?"

She looked to see if he were mocking her again. His face gave nothing away. He's a controlled one, she thought, fighting down another flutter of nerves. Is Kildrurry really worth all this? The memory of her father instantly quelled the doubt. John MacKay was worth it.

"My work is quite varied, actually," she said, fixing what she hoped was a professional look on her face. "The business has become sort of a hodgepodge of old methods combined with the new. Usually I get a—feeling. It's difficult to describe. I seem to know intuitively if something's there."

He cocked a brow. "You mean you're psychic?"

"No, although I wish I were. Some people say it's an acquired ability or at least one you can cultivate with time and hard work. I'm inclined to believe that you either have it or you don't. In my case, I don't go much beyond tingles and goose bumps."

"Very scientific," he commented dryly.

"They merely set the stage," she replied a bit testily. "Actually I have a rather complicated set of psychological and physical tests that I run before I attempt to make any determination in a case."

"I see." He gave her a long direct look. "And that's the technique you plan to use here at Burke House?"

"Initially, at least. I've found that it's best to handle each case individually. What works under one set of circumstances is liable to be useless under another."

"And yet the basis of scientific procedure is the ability to repeat an experiment while obtaining the same results." He paused as he regarded her over the rim of his glass. "You did profess to be a scientist, didn't you, Miss Ramsey?"

The man was absolutely infuriating! He seemed to know just which buttons to press to get her goat. "As a scientist I find it difficult to reject a discovery simply because it can't be explained or necessarily repeated under sterile laboratory conditions. Psychic phenomena are no more inexplicable than say, perception or memory."

He'd watched her struggle for control with interest. He noticed that her hands were smooth and that she moved them expressively when she talked, especially when she was angry. Her fingers were long and well formed, yet she wore no rings and her nails were short and unpolished. She was obviously intelligent, with a far better than average education, yet she had chosen to dedicate her life to hunting ghosts. Athena Ramsey appeared to be a very contradictory young lady.

"Did you know that your eyes turn a musky gold when you're angry?" he said unexpectedly.

His change of subject nearly threw Athena off balance. "I fail to see what the color of my eyes has to do with scientific procedure." Good Lord, she was a trained professional. Kildrurry or not, she didn't have to put up with this!

"Am I to assume that since I've been invited to Burke House you've decided not to act on your skepticism?" she asked him bluntly.

"I'd say that's a fair assumption."

"Then you're planning to give me a free hand?"

"Not at all."

"But you just said—"

"I said that I would allow you to remain in Burke House, Miss Ramsey," he interrupted. "That invitation does not imply carte blanche. Within reason, I will permit you to carry out your so-called experiments. Anything beyond that remains to be seen."

He drained his drink and placed it behind him on the mantel. When he turned back there was a new hardness in his eyes. "It's important that you understand the situation," he went on. "You see, I'm very fond of my grandmother, and as far as possible, I try to go along with her wishes. However, she is getting old and, as I mentioned before, she's in failing health. While I'm willing to humor her, I can't allow her to be upset by this business."

He walked over and took Athena's empty glass. As he did, his fingers lingered lightly on hers, and he so towered over her that she was forced to bend her head backward to look up at him. She felt a slight vertigo and was once again far too aware of his closeness.

"I trust I make myself clear."

The contract of his hand on hers was electric. Athena felt the sharp tingle and barely resisted the urge to pull away from him. Her senses were acutely tuned to him as her anger rapidly turned into another emotion that was far more difficult to analyze. From the faint tremor of her hand inside his, she decided it had to be fear. Christopher Burke was an intimidating man. Who wouldn't be afraid?

Or excited? the persistent little voice pointed out. Or fascinated?

Athena swallowed hard, pushing these thoughts from her mind. "Yes," she answered him, aware that her voice was slightly hoarse. "You've made yourself perfectly clear."

His gaze didn't waver from hers. "Good. I'm sure neither of us would want to be responsible for a setback in her condition." He released her hand and watched her pull it quickly behind her back. Her face was pale, although her eyes had not dropped from his. "Shall we go in to dinner now?"

"Athena. That's an unusual name."

They were sitting at a refectory table in one of the largest dining rooms Athena had ever seen. A fire blazed at one end of the room, while a Gobelin tapestry formed the backdrop for a collection of antique Scottish artifacts at the other. The table was set with fine old china and lit by a five-tier chandelier.

Since they'd moved out of the library, Christopher had been the perfect host. Beneath the correctly cool exterior, however, Athena sensed his continued reserve toward her. In defense, she'd decided to ignore his vague aloofness and, as much as possible, enjoy the excellent meal. He could only irritate her if she allowed him, she reasoned. Athena resolved not to give him the satisfaction.

"My mother teaches high school Latin as well as Greek and Roman mythology," she told him pleasantly. "I have a brother called Apollo and a younger sister who's struggled with the name Artemis for the past twenty-four years." She looked around the huge dining room. "Do you ever eat in the kitchen? Now that your grandmother's confined to her room you must rattle around in here."

"Mary, our cook, would never allow the invasion to her kitchen." He paused while Fiona took their plates. "Are your brother and sister in equally—unusual professions?"

She smiled at him, this time determined not to let him bait her. "My brother's a dentist in Ohio, my sister has a degree in accounting. She and her husband are expecting their first child next month. They would consider 'unusual' a tame description for what I do. They think I'm completely off the wall."

He looked puzzled. "Off the wall?"

"You know, kooky—strange."

"Ah, yes." Lachlan entered unobtrusively carrying a platter of baked salmon. "This is freshly caught," Christopher told her. "There are some compensations to living on the North Sea." His words were punctuated by a dimming of the lights and a clap of thunder. Athena couldn't help laughing at his somber expression. "I'm relieved that you're taking our inclement weather in stride, Miss Ramsey," he continued.

"Please. 'Miss Ramsey' makes me feel like someone's maiden aunt. Call me Athena."

He nodded slightly. "If you'd prefer."

She studied him as he cut into the salmon. Despite his size, his movements were smooth, almost graceful. His body was so lean and firmly muscled that Athena wondered if he kept in shape by actively helping to construct his own projects. His deeply tanned skin led her to believe this was a real possibility. In spite of his churlish personality, she had to admit she liked the way his brown complexion contrasted with his reddish-blond hair and blue eyes.

"I think I'd even feel safe from a hurricane in here," she went on, deciding that the fish was delicious. "Burke House looks strong enough to withstand a full-fledged invasion."

"It's withstood several over the centuries." He poured more wine into her glass, then watched her face as she took a sip. She looked up to meet his gaze and he read intelligence and good humor in her eyes—and too much perception. "More potatoes?" he asked, deliberately breaking the moment. There was more to Athena Ramsey than met the eye, he decided, letting the rest of dinner pass in thoughtful silence. Perhaps she would be more of a challenge than he'd anticipated.

"Thank you, Lachlan," Christopher told the butler as the dour man carried their coffee and dessert into the library. Christopher nodded to the chairs in front of the fire, and the butler placed the tray on the table between them.

Silently Lachlan poured coffee into two cups, then uncovered a plate of oatmeal and gingerbread that Christopher called "broonies." Athena took a taste and found it delicious. The coffee, too, was excellent—strong, but hot and very rich. Still, Athena was finding it difficult to continue the game she'd been playing with herself since dinner. The man sitting beside her made game playing of any kind very difficult indeed!

He was simply too overpowering a presence to take lightly. Even seated casually in the chair next to hers, one long muscular leg crossed negligently over the other, he seemed larger than life. Since she'd met Christopher earlier this evening, the built-in antennae that inevitably warned Athena of impending danger had scarcely let up. She felt as if she was engaged in a subtle, psychological battle, a contest of wills. And against what odds? she wondered. Realistically, what sort of chance did she have against a man like Christopher Burke?

Athena stole a glance at his strong, straight profile and the shock of strawberry-blond hair that had fallen across his forehead. She knew he was only thirty-seven, but the lines of bitterness around his eyes and mouth made him look older. What had happened to put those lines there? she mused. He held himself under such rigid restraint. Why? What was Christopher Burke really like?

"Why don't you tell me about your grandmother's ghost?" she asked, steering her mind back to business. His personal life mattered only insofar as it affected her mission here, she reminded herself. She couldn't afford to be sidetracked.

A crash of thunder rattled the windows. Christopher watched her glance over her shoulder, then back to him. Rather than being frightened, she seemed pleased with the weather.

"I love a good rain," she said, sensing the direction of his thoughts. "As long as I'm warm and dry and sitting in front of the fire. And a storm at Burke House seems particularly fitting."

"You sound like a romantic, Miss Ramsey. In this part of Scotland, storms are not looked upon as favors from the gods."

"Athena, remember?" Did he ever smile? she wondered. Was this another indication of how much he resented her presence at Burke House, or did he treat all people this way? "Guilty, I'm afraid. There is a touch of the romantic in me. But I've always thought it made life more interesting—more like an adventure."

"Most romantics I've known simply haven't experienced enough of the real world," he commented dryly.

"My, my, such pessimism." She smiled as she sipped her coffee. "Does life really have to be so serious? Can't there be room for the unexpected?"

"I do my best to avoid the unexpected." His side glance at her belied the impersonal nature of his words. "I've always found it best to be prepared."

She smiled nervously. Frequently Athena was able to "tune" in to people—to get a sense of their feelings and moods, often their fears. Although she had nothing as precise or developed as extrasensory perception, her sensitivity had nonetheless proved very helpful to her in her work.

Christopher Burke remained a blank slate. The only "feelings" she received about him were purely external. They could just as easily have been deduced from what she'd already learned about him before arriving at Burke House. The inner man remained a mystery. It was as if he had the ability to pull a protective shield over his thoughts, enabling him to see out but allowing no one else to see in. Athena simply couldn't sort him out, and because he continued to be an enigma her job at Burke House was made that much more difficult.

She put her coffee back onto the table between them and said tactfully, "You have to admit that a storm does create a wonderful atmosphere for telling ghost stories." She paused for a single heartbeat. "Tell me about Angus MacKay."

Christopher looked at her in silence, then finished his coffee and placed it next to hers on the table. She'd slipped out of her boots and was curled up in the chair watching him. He gazed back into the fire as he remembered the stories from his childhood. Most of them had been told to him by his grandmother. He barely remembered his mother. And she would not have been the type to tell nursery stories at any rate.

"Gram didn't tell you the legend, then?" he asked, studying her face in the firelight.

"A few details in her letters, but very sketchy. I didn't want to tire her this afternoon."

"I see."

Something in his tone bothered Athena. Did he suspect her motives in asking? "Being a skeptic, I thought you'd be more likely to tell the story objectively."

"And you're interested in objectivity."

Athena couldn't help the small hairs that once again rose on the back of her neck. "Always," she answered smoothly. "I'm a scientist, remember?"

His look was coolly measured. "Yes, so you've told me."

"You *do* know the story," she persisted, ignoring the barb.

"Every Burke knows the story," he said, holding her eyes. "I would imagine that every MacKay knows it as well," he added slowly.

She could have sworn that he put particular emphasis on these last words, then the moment was gone leaving her to hope she had imagined it.

Don't let your nerves get to you, she told herself firmly. Don't blow it now!

"I really would like to hear the story," she asked again.

Christopher's cool blue eyes assessed her for another long moment. A log broke on the fire and the grandfather's clock in the corner dramatically struck ten times. Outside, she could hear the steady clatter of rain hitting the windows. Aside from that, the house was very silent.

"All right," he agreed at last. With a little start, Athena realized she'd been holding her breath. "If you're that determined to hear it, I'll tell you the story of Angus MacKay."

Three

———

Whether it was a trick of the storm or a distortion of her own jangled nerves, Christopher's voice seemed to completely fill the quiet room. She looked at him briefly, then feared that her thoughts might be too easy to read. What would his version of the MacKay myth be like? She'd heard it so many times from her father. How would it sound coming from a Burke?

"According to the legend," he began slowly, fixing her with his direct, disturbing gaze, "the MacKays and the Burkes had been feuding for generations. In those days it wasn't uncommon for border clans to attack one another just as fiercely as they took on the British. In the case of the MacKay and Burke clans, the hostilities were particularly intense since they occupied adjoining lands. Night raids between the two were common, and over the years countless lives were lost in the periodic skirmishes."

He paused and poured fresh coffee into their cups. Athena didn't move. He made it sound so casual, this feud between their families. Would that be his tack? she wondered. Would he understate the significance of what happened between the MacKays and the Burkes all those years ago?

"In 1634," he resumed, "whether out of desperation or dwindling resources, the leader of the MacKay clan proposed an end to their hostilities. In order to celebrate the new peace, the Burkes invited their old enemies to have dinner at Burke House—probably in the very room we dined in tonight. It was Christmas Eve, so the story goes." He looked at her in the firelight. "An auspicious time to make peace."

"Yes," she answered softly, thinking of the awful irony. Christmas Eve, a night for brotherly love and goodwill— not deception. Yet it was under just such a cloud of treachery that the MacKays made their ill-fated journey to Burke House on that holiest of nights.

Christopher continued to study Athena's face. Her eyes were very wide and seemed to be a dark, reddish-gold color now. Were they reflecting the fire, he wondered, or her thoughts?

"My ancestors weren't particularly trusting fellows," he went on. "And for good reason, as it turned out. Just in case the MacKays had something other than peace up their sleeves, the Burkes decided they'd best be prepared."

Prepared for what? Athena thought angrily. Mass slaughter? She forced down a growing feeling of resentment. "Wasn't the fact that dinner was to be held inside their own fortress defense enough?" she asked, unable to completely hide her feelings.

"Border claims didn't survive in those days by being chivalrous," he told her dryly. "Burke knew enough to arm himself and the others who would be at the table, and to station sentries at key points around the castle where they would be ready for any eventuality.''

"How hospitable of them. The MacKays didn't have much of a chance, did they?''

"As much of a chance as they were willing to give the Burkes,'' he countered calmly. "According to the story, old Angus MacKay had his own contingent of men waiting in the woods outside the castle.''

"With Burke's men watching their every move.''

"Trying their best, I'm sure.''

He paused for a moment to look into the fire, and Athena realized that despite all her efforts to remain emotionally uninvolved her nerves were like tightly coiled springs ready to snap. How could he sit there and speak so calmly of his ancestor's betrayal? She closed her eyes and felt the terrible oppressiveness settling upon her again. Was that what she'd been experiencing since she'd arrived at Burke House? After 350 years, was that violent night still inexorably etched into the memory of the castle?

She sensed he was waiting for her reaction before going on. *Be careful, Athena,* a small voice cautioned. Bracing herself for what she knew would follow, she asked, "What happened?''

He continued to look at her for a long moment without a flicker of expression. Athena wondered if something in her voice, or her face, had given her away. She could feel her heart pound erratically as she waited for him to go on.

Christopher found it interesting to watch the flow of emotions across the smooth planes of her face. All evening he'd tried to ignore her beauty as an unnecessary complication to his plans. Still, he continued to be intrigued by the woman, a sobering fact that would have to be dealt with later.

"The first part of the evening passed smoothly enough," he went on. "Then one of the leaders, no one knows which, proposed a game of chance."

Athena's eyes flew open in surprise. "A game of chance?" This was a twist in the story she hadn't expected. "You mean a game of cards, or dice?"

He raised a brow. "Does it make a difference?"

Athena recovered quickly, angry she was finding it so difficult to control her emotions. "Of course not. I was just curious." Irritated at herself, she reached for her coffee. "Go on. Please."

Still watching her, he said, "As the game progressed, I imagine too many drinks were consumed, and the stakes became increasingly high. Finally the entire holdings of the two clans were riding on one throw of the dice."

A log cracked sharply on the fire, and Athena started at the sudden noise. She leaned back in her chair, forcing her shoulders to relax. "And—?"

He gave a slight shrug of his shoulders. "Angus MacKay lost. Furious at his defeat, he gave the signal that alerted the secret troops he'd stationed around the castle. If he couldn't defeat his old enemy honestly, he was prepared to resort to more drastic measures."

"How can you be sure of that?" she demanded. "How can you possibly know that Angus MacKay gave the signal first?"

"You really do take these things seriously, don't you? It's a legend, remember? A ghost story for a stormy night."

"But it's a story with some basis in truth, isn't it?" she challenged. "Historically, the Burkes did take over the MacKay holdings that night."

"You make it sound as if they stole them. MacKay lost everything in a game of chance."

"According to you."

His expression remained maddeningly calm. "And others." He nodded toward the large book she'd examined earlier. "If you're interested, the events are recorded in the clan register over there—the book you were looking at before dinner." He paused and she thought he was enjoying her distress. "You *were* reading about the MacKays when I came in, weren't you, Athena? I must have interrupted you before you could get to the most interesting part of the story—the section that details how Angus MacKay gambled away his estate that night."

Athena's eyes had flown to the book. "It's actually written in there?"

"Every word." He motioned to the bookcase behind the stand, grim amusement mirrored in his eyes. "There's an entire section over there devoted to Scottish history. Since you seem such a devoted student, you might be interested."

Athena sat back in her chair. In her father's version of the story there'd been no mention of gambling between the two clans. There'd been only deception—and the most brutal kind of betrayal. Tomorrow she would have to see Christopher's supposed evidence. The resolution brought Athena a new fear. What if she found it? After all these years, what would she do if she discovered her father had been wrong?

"Yes," she said vaguely, her mind still trying to come to grips with this disturbing thought. "I'll . . . I'll be sure to look them over while I'm here." He was still watching her, a considering look on his angular face. Athena straightened and met his gaze. "And so they fought," she prompted, anxious now for the story, and the evening, to be over.

"Yes, they fought." He saw that mention of the clan chronicle had sown a seed of doubt. Absently he speculated on what sort of fruit it would bear. "Although I'm not sure that it was much of a contest. The Burkes were ready for them, and not only did they have the element of surprise, they were thoroughly familiar with the castle and its terrain. It must have been over quickly. According to the story, there were few MacKays left. Those who weren't killed outright were either captured or fled into the night."

Athena caught her breath as she sensed the terrible violence of that night. So many lives lost—her family, the people of Kildrurry. She felt as if she knew them now—she could feel their anger and their awful suffering. How many made the fateful journey to Burke House that Christmas Eve? How few returned?

"The story really has upset you."

His voice jarred into her thoughts, and she realized that she'd been lost once again in the past. Athena looked up at him angrily. "Of course it's upset me. I find it hard to believe you can sit there speaking about it so calmly. It seems a remarkably senseless way for all those men to die."

"And you think one way of dying is more sensible than another?"

"It can be honorable. It can have some kind of meaning."

"You're a dreamer, Athena."

"I'm a human being, Christopher," she shot back. "And I can't help mourning any pointless loss of human life!"

"Even when it happened over three centuries ago?"

"Even if it happened three *thousand* years ago!" Disregarding her boots, which were still lying beneath the chair, she stood and paced to the fire, pivoting on the sealskin rug to confront him. "Don't you see? We're all bound together—time is meaningless, relative only to our current frame of reference. To claim that pointless human slaughter no longer matters simply because it took place in another time or space is to ignore our cosmic relationship to each other."

"Cosmic relationship," he repeated blankly. "What is that, some kind of psychic mumbo jumbo?"

She stared at him in angry frustration. "You haven't understood one word I've said, have you?"

"Speak the queen's English and I might." He rose from the chair, and as his muscular form reached its full height, Athena was again much too aware of his towering menace. "You can't really take all that nonsense seriously."

"Nonsense!" A fresh wave of resentment swept all thoughts of caution from her mind. "Is that all it is to you, nonsense?" she accused. "Those people—the Mac-Kays—they were living, breathing human beings. They had their dreams, too, just like you and I. And families—all those men who were killed, the ones you dismiss so casually, they had wives and children and parents. Can you imagine how they must have felt when their husbands or sons or fathers didn't come home that night—that Christmas Eve? *Christmas Eve,* Christopher! And then the final indignity—to be driven from their home by the very men who had brutally murdered their kin. Christopher, think of it! Are you so lacking in feeling that you can't see what it must have been like for—"

` A crack of thunder drowned out her words and she stopped abruptly, only then realizing she'd been shouting. Athena felt her face drain of color, then flush red with embarrassment. What was she doing? Where was her control, her objectivity? How much had she given away?

Disconcerted, Athena moved back to her chair and hastily began pulling on one of her boots. "Sorry," she muttered. "I guess I got carried away."

"I thought scientists were supposed to remain objective."

Something in his tone made her risk a quick look at him. Once again he'd come entirely too close to reading her thoughts. "I'm also a human being," she murmured, yanking on the other boot. "And I find it a very disturbing story."

"But one that you were most insistent on hearing." He watched thoughtfully as she zipped up the second boot. "I wonder why?"

This time her eyes flew to his. "I wanted to know what I was up against, that's all. Before starting an investigation, I try to gather as many facts as possible."

"And what about your...intuition, Athena?" he persisted softly. "You said you were only human. What do your feelings tell you?"

She stood, avoiding his face, wanting to get away from the room, from him. But it was too late. With a grace remarkable for his size, he had already moved to stand in front of her. She had no choice but to look up into those granite eyes. He stood there above her, poised, waiting.

And what *do* your feelings tell you, Athena? she thought helplessly. That you came here unprepared? That you had no idea you could care so much about people who lived more than three centuries ago? That you want to get back at this man for being a Burke—for what he and all the Burkes before him did to your family, to your father? That in spite of everything, all that happened that still hasn't been set right, you still can't help being aware of him in the most fundamental, the most feminine way possible?

"It's late," she forced herself to tell him evenly. "It's been an...an interesting evening, but I'm still suffering from jet lag." She managed a weak smile. "If you don't mind, I'd like to turn in now."

Before she could move away from him, he reached out and took her arm. The power of his grip made Athena start. She tried to free her arm from the manacle of his hand, but she might just as well have attempted to disengage herself from a vise.

Light from the fire played across on his face, and once again she had the dizzying sensation of slipping backward in time. In the dancing shadows he loomed above her like a golden Viking, intensely exciting and just as frightening. She felt rooted to the spot, mesmerized. Even if he hadn't had such an iron-hard grip on her arm, she doubted she would have had the ability to move.

"You're afraid, Athena," he said, moving his face very close to hers. "I want to know why. Surely it can't be ghosts. I wonder...could it be you're afraid of me?"

"Don't be ridiculous." She hated the unsteady note in her voice. "I'm just tired—I told you."

"Yes, it was a long trip. A very long journey to look for a ghost, wasn't it, Athena? Even one as fascinating as Angus MacKay."

His voice was deceptively calm, belying the dangerous gleam she saw lighting the clear, icy blue eyes. His free hand went to her waist and tightened. She felt the hard grip of his fingers through her wool dress. Athena waited breathlessly for what he might do, but he'd gone very still above her. His voice was a hoarse whisper above the wailing wind outside. "You wouldn't have had something else in mind when you came to Scotland, would you, Athena?"

They seemed to stand there for an eternity, then thunder once again shook the windows and Christopher felt a physical release. He heard her exhale softly as she turned away, breaking contact with his hand. Slowly he relaxed his muscles, only then realizing how much effort it had cost him not to pull her into his arms.

"You're right, it's late," he said shortly, turning toward the door. "I'll show you to your room."

Athena did not get undressed immediately. The room, she told herself, was too cold, but she knew the real reason was her restlessness. She poked at the listless fire, then went to stand by the window. Outside, the rain swept down in torrents, several times hardening into marbles of hail that pelted the panes with such force she feared they would break.

It was turbulent, she thought, just like her emotions. Dear God, what had she let herself in for? This was not what she'd expected when she promised her father to visit Scotland. Psychic phenomena she could handle. And she couldn't deny she was intrigued by a 350-year-old ghost. But Christopher Burke! Athena shivered. No, he was much, much more than she'd bargained for!

Angrily she released the drapes. Why was she letting him get to her like this? If it was a battle they were engaged in, he'd already won the first skirmish hands down. How much did he suspect? Athena shook her head in frustration. It was so difficult to tell. The man gave away nothing.

All right, she thought, pulling a flannel nightgown out of the drawer. If it was going to be a contest of wills she'd have to be better prepared next time. Just how much did she know about Christopher Burke? While she undressed she mentally ticked off the meager information she'd been able to collect about the man before leaving the States.

He was the elder of two sons and had excelled in school and sports, both in Scotland and later, when he'd attended Oxford. She knew his mother had disappeared sometime before his tenth birthday, but whether the woman had died or had simply left her husband, she'd been unable to discover. In fact, Athena had been able to unearth very little else about Christopher's life until his father's death a decade ago when he'd taken over Burke Enterprises. Since that time, he'd been in the news more frequently, but even then the stories rarely dealt with the man's private affairs.

As a businessman, he was rapidly establishing a reputation as a shrewd and innovative entrepreneur. In the decade since he'd taken over Burke Enterprises, the company had nearly doubled in size, diversifying and significantly broadening its scope of operation.

She knew there'd been an early marriage, but here, too, the details were sketchy, ending in yet another mysterious disappearance. What had happened to his wife? she wondered. She seemed to have slipped off the face of the earth—much as Christopher's mother had years before.

All of which told her next to nothing about the man, she realized in frustration. What lay behind the hard glint in those icy blue eyes? What made him tick? What was he really like?

"Brr." Athena shivered as she came into icy contact with the sheets. She curled her legs against her body for warmth. "Get to sleep before you turn into an icicle."

But sleep eluded her. Propped up on the pillows, she watched the coals from the hearth glow red in the darkness as she thought again of the scene in the library. He'd wanted to kiss her—she was sure of it. What had held him back? And how would she have reacted if he had? She stared into the fire and remembered the feel of his hand on her waist, the clean, musky scent that had nearly over-whelmed her senses. What would it have been like in his arms? Would his lips have been warm and inviting or hard and uncompromising like his eyes?

Good Lord! With a grunt of self-disgust, Athena turned over onto her stomach, pounding her fist hard into the pillow. Enough of ghosts and legends. Certainly enough of Christopher Burke! Pull up the covers, close your eyes and go to sleep. Tomorrow is going to be a very busy day!

After leaving Athena at her door, Christopher did not go directly to his room. Too restive to sleep, he went in-stead to his study. It was a sanctuary few people saw; the one room Fiona and Lachlan were not allowed to touch.

He walked to the grate and stirred the embers of a dying fire, urged it to life again, then tossed on a fresh log. He had a great deal of work to do—preliminary plans for the golf course waited to be examined, the new shopping mall in Glasgow was nearing completion and next week they would break ground for the new government complex in Petershead. Yet as he sat behind his desk, it was Athena he thought of, not the papers in front of him.

She shouldn't intrigue me, he thought. Women were a distraction he had long since put out of his life. And this woman was as deadly—no, deadlier—than most. The Trojan horse, he thought grimly, the female wolf in sheep's clothing. He'd allowed her to penetrate his lair. It had seemed tactical at the time. Now he wondered.

Christopher pushed aside his papers and reached for a folder that documented the twenty-seven and a half years of Athena Ramsey Mackay's life. He remembered her brief, nearly honest, autobiography at dinner, then

thought of the details he could have added—political af-
filiations, school grades, boyfriends, shoe size, credit rat-
ing. But though he was aware of how close she'd been to
her father, Christopher knew next to nothing about her
thoughts, her fears, her feelings, in short, about Athena
MacKay, the woman.

He pushed aside the file, disturbed. No, the last thing
she should do is intrigue me. Forewarned should mean
forearmed. I know what she's up to; it would be stupid and
costly to let her think she might get away with it.

Yet only moments ago he had very nearly kissed her.
And he couldn't deny that given the opportunity, it would
be difficult to resist the temptation to make love to her.
Perhaps it had simply been too long since he'd had a
woman. He might close off his mind and his heart, but biological needs could not be so easily ignored. But why *this*
woman? He hadn't felt this way for nearly ten years. Not
since Sylvia.

Christopher suppressed the anger he always felt when he
thought of his ex-wife. Where were they, he wondered—
Rome, Paris? When last he'd heard, they'd been living in
London. Ryan must be doing well, he thought dryly. But
then that's what they both wanted—travel, excitement.

With a muttered curse, Christopher pushed back his
chair. It was useless trying to work tonight. Stacking his
notes, he got up and pulled the fireplace screen across the
grate. He was reaching for the light switch when he heard
the scream.

Athena wakened with a start. For a moment she sat up
in bed disoriented, then the sound was repeated. Someone
was screaming. It was coming from a slight distance away,
but the voice was high and shrill enough to carry. With a
shiver of alarm, Athena realized it was Gram.

Somehow she found her way through the maze of hallway to the second-floor landing. Below, she saw Christopher bending over what looked like a pile of blue cloth. Then the cloth moved and Athena saw Gram's face, stark white, eyes wide with fear.

"What happened?" she asked him, flying down the last few stairs.

"I don't know. Somehow she got out of her room and fell."

Athena was shocked to see the fear in his eyes. The master of Burke House had a chink in his armor after all. And it was a tiny, vulnerable, eighty-three-year-old woman!

"She's shaken, but other than that she seems to be all right," he went on. "I'm going to get her back to bed."

Lifting her as effortlessly as if she were a doll, Christopher carried the woman back into her room and placed her gently on the bed. With great tenderness he pulled back the covers and tucked her carefully beneath the sheets. Athena thought Gram looked pathetically small and fragile in the large bed. Only her faded blue eyes looked alert, and they were watching Athena anxiously. "What happened, Gram?" Athena asked her softly.

"It was that devil, Angus MacKay," the old woman said, her voice weak but angry. "I thought I'd catch him at it for once, so you'd have something to start with tomorrow. But my miserable legs gave right out from under me."

"Does he do this often, Gram?" Athena asked her.

Out of the corner of her eye, she caught Christopher's glare of disapproval. Before he could object, Clara Burke answered.

"Often enough to put these gray hairs in me head." Her voice dropped to a whisper. "'Tis always the same...his footsteps comin' down the hall until they stop at my door. Just stop—not another sound.'' Her eyes were very large as they pleaded with Athena. "But he's there. I know he's there—just waitin'.''

"Waiting for what, Gram?" Christopher asked her gently. "Why would old Angus want to frighten you like that?"

"What difference does it make why? He's there and he's got to be stopped." She started to raise off the pillow, and Christopher reached out an arm to keep her quiet. Gram leaned back, but her eyes continued to bore into Athena. "You'll stop him, won't you, lass? You gave me your word!"

"Calm down, Gram," Christopher told her softly. "You must have had a bad dream. It's all right now."

"It's not all right as well you'd know if you'd been here," she told her grandson sharply. "It's high time the old scoundrel was stopped." She reached for Athena's hand. "You'll start tomorrow. You promised."

"Yes, Gram, I promise," Athena agreed soothingly. "I'll start first thing in the morning."

The old woman looked at her for a long moment, then sank back onto the pillow, exhausted. "Tomorrow," she sighed, closing her eyes.

"I told you I don't want her hurt," Christopher said tightly as they walked up the stairs.

"And you think that I do?" Athena answered through chattering teeth. Now that the shock of Gram's fall had subsided, Athena realized that in her haste to get downstairs she'd come out of her room dressed only in her nightgown and slippers. She was very nearly freezing. "Has it ever occurred to you that you may do more harm than good by ignoring the problem?"

"My grandmother's very old. And very superstitious."

"Come on, Christopher," she said in frustration. "You can't still maintain it's her imagination."

"What else can it be? Certainly not a ghost!"

"Ah, yes," she replied, too tired and cold to mask her sarcasm. "The practical Christopher Burke. Unless it can be seen and heard and touched it doesn't exist."

Tiny lines of anger formed around his eyes, but Athena was too lost in her own frustration to notice. "Let's just say I've outgrown fairy tales," he told her shortly.

Athena whirled around to face him as they stopped at her door. "Fairy tales? That's how you chose to explain your grandmother's torment? What a very convenient way to avoid your own responsibility in the matter."

The skin stretched tautly across Christopher's face. "I don't need you to remind me of my responsibilities," he told her with icy restraint.

Athena remained oblivious to the danger signals being telegraphed by his darkening eyes, concern for Gram taking precedence over caution. "Oh, really? Well, permit me to explain a few simple facts. What your grandmother is experiencing is very real. I saw love—honest caring—in your eyes a few minutes ago. Yet you're willing to hide your head in the sand while a poor old woman is terrorized by a force you're too *practical* to recognize." She reached for the handle to her door. "Unfortunately for her, you may live to regret your narrow-mindedness."

His hand closed over hers before she could turn the knob, but Athena held her ground. "Are you going to tell me to leave Burke House?" she challenged. "Is that what comes next? I'd think twice about that if I were you, Christopher. I'm the only one who may be able to help your grandmother."

"Help her—or *you*?" His hand tightened on hers, and she felt a stab of pain as the doorknob dug into her palm.

His other arm moved around her waist, jerking her around until she faced him. "Are you going to tell me that's why you came here, Athena? To purge my grandmother of her demons? Is that why you were so interested in Angus MacKay's story? Or was there a more personal reason?"

In one fluid movement he crushed her into the steel-hard surface of his chest. Athena gasped and felt her heart pound beneath her nightgown. She tried to twist out of his arms but it was useless. With a stab of fear, she realized she was completely at the mercy of his superior strength. Looking up at the blue fire burning in those hard eyes, she found the knowledge extremely disturbing.

"Tell me why you came here, Athena?" he demanded hoarsely. "I want to hear you say it. Why, after three hundred years has a MacKay come back to Burke House?"

Athena's heart stopped beating. Before she could respond, his arms choked off any chance of a denial. In a fog of confusion, she had time to register the gripping power of his embrace and the flashing, cold blue eyes before his face closed down on her.

There was nothing gentle about the kiss. It was hungry and totally possessive from the first touch of his lips. Caught off guard, Athena could only cling to him as if her life depended upon it. It was like clinging to a rock. His body was hard, his lips unrelenting. He invaded, he ravaged, he plundered.

When his hand closed on her breast she shuddered, too dizzy to analyze the electricity he sent searing through her body. Long skillful fingers burned her flesh into exciting awareness. He pulled her against his thighs and she felt his taut and demanding body. Energy pulsed through the pair, binding them in a way Athena had never before experienced. It terrified her. It thrilled her!

She tried to force herself to stand still. If she couldn't escape, she would at least remain passive to his assault. But the probing, seeking pressure of his hands would not permit such a defense. His tongue explored deeper into the dark, sweet recesses of her mouth. She wanted to hate him for the intimacy, but felt only an agony of pleasure. Without her permission, her hands ran up his back until they were gripping the hard mountains of his shoulders. Here was danger. Here was an excitement the likes of which she had never known. She shivered as his tongue moved triumphantly, possessively, through the territory it had so boldly staked.

When the fine line of sanity would be crossed, he released her. As he stood looking down at her, she saw anger and frustration in the dark depths of his eyes. "Is it only ghosts you've come for, Athena MacKay?" he demanded. "Or is it something else you're after?"

A crash of thunder shook the walls as he turned from her. Too shocked to speak, she stared after him as his long strides carried him quickly down the hallway and out of sight.

For a long time Athena didn't move. Then, quietly, she entered her room, closing the door soundlessly behind her.

Four

Athena watched the falling snow from her bedroom window. It might be April, yet the smooth white blanket that surrounded the castle on three sides was nearly a foot deep. Fiona was right after all. North Berwick did not consider itself bound by anything as conventional as a calendar!

At breakfast Athena felt alone and ridiculous in the oversize dining room, as Fiona served her eggs and toast and informed her that Christopher had managed to get out earlier in his Land Rover four-wheel drive. Athena knew the small European compact she'd rented wouldn't make it as far as the road. With a sinking feeling, she realized she was stuck at Burke House.

Finishing her coffee, she thought again of her inexplicable host. By the light of day she'd been able to put the ridiculous notion of Christopher as a medieval Viking firmly out of her mind. The castle had too much atmosphere, she decided, resolving not to fall prey again to an overactive imagination. Christopher might be overwhelming, but he was, after all, just a man—and a twentieth-century one at that. She'd handled difficult men before. If he thought he could scare her off by using strong-arm tactics, he was badly mistaken. Until he came right out and asked her to leave Burke House, she had every intention of getting on with her job.

Leaving the dining room, Athena headed for the library. First order of the day was to examine Christopher's so-called evidence supporting his version of the MacKay-Burke feud.

She approached the large old clan register with a mixture of trepidation and excitement. Christopher had seemed so sure of himself. Could he really have proof? Carefully she paged back through the old book to the section on Clan MacKay. Well, she thought, we'll soon see.

She read the archaic script through twice, then once again for good measure. In places the wording was difficult to decipher, but the meaning was clear. There, as an adjunct to the family history, was Christopher's evidence. On Christmas Eve, in 1634, the MacKays had lost Kildrurry, along with the remainder of their clan holdings, to the Burkes of North Berwick. *In a game of chance.*

Athena felt a chill that had nothing to do with the drafty room. Could it be possible? she asked herself numbly. Could Dad have been that mistaken? She thought back, trying to remember if her father had ever mentioned having proof of his own, something to substantiate three centuries of purported injustice. There had been endless stories of Burke treachery, of course, heated tales told at clan gatherings for as far back as she could remember. But did these constitute proof, or were they based on hearsay and wishful thinking?

Surely it was more than that! Her father might have been a dreamer, but even he must have based a lifelong obsession on something more substantial than old stories.

Athena closed the book with a little bang. Proof or not, the only thing to do now was to get on with her investigation. She still felt strongly that there was something here, that the answer lay hidden at Burke House. All right then, it was up to her to find it!

Returning to her room, Athena went over to the boxes containing her equipment. Last night the instruments had been carried upstairs, but otherwise they'd been left untouched in a corner of the bedroom. Going through them now, she decided to follow her usual procedure in a case like this—she would do her best to eliminate any possibility of delusion or fraud, then she would detect and measure as much of the supposed physical events and energies as she could.

Carrying the first of the boxes downstairs, she decided her best bet was to set up outside Gram's room, the "hot spot" of the psychic activity. Almost immediately she was joined by the old woman. Attracted by the noises Athena was making in the hall, Mrs. Burke maneuvered her wheelchair out of her bedroom with surprising agility, then sat watching the younger woman with sharp inquisitiveness.

"What are you doin' with those gadgets?" she asked as Athena set up several photocells at strategic locations along the walls.

"I'm going to test for light," Athena told her patiently. "Very often an apparition is accompanied by electromagnetic radiation." She smiled at Gram's bewilderment. "It's a kind of light," she went on, "a luminescence. If I can detect light of that kind, then we've got something to go on."

"My, my, lassie," the old woman said, shaking her head. "What will they think of next?" She watched Athena keenly. "And what's that you're attachin' to it?"

"It's a polygraph—to record the readings. When I turn it on, paper will run through the machine while tiny pens mark down any changes in the instruments."

Gram nodded in amazement, then watched silently for a few minutes. When Athena brought a second box down from her room, she asked, "And those? What plans do you have in mind for those doohickeys?"

"These are thermistors," Athena explained. "They're like thermometers. Hopefully they'll tell us if your ghost comes with a 'cold spot,' you know, a kind of chill."

Gram thought about this for a moment. "Now that you mention it, I do remember it feelin' draftier than usual when the old devil is about." She chuckled dryly. "Of course around here a body would be hard pressed to say that one part of the house is colder than another."

By the time Athena was finished setting up for her first set of readings, it was time for lunch. Rather than go through another session alone in the dining room, she suggested that she eat with Gram in her bedroom. The old woman seemed delighted with the suggestion.

Stoically Lachlan set up a table in front of the window where he silently served them a light lunch consisting of soup and some thin meat sandwiches. If the elderly butler resented having to carry an extra set of dishes up to his mistress's room, he gave no indication whatsoever.

"Do you think you'll get somethin' out of all those gadgets then, lass?" Gram asked as she made her way through the meal with remarkably good appetite.

"If something's there, I should get a reading," Athena assured her. "When I've finished testing for light and temperature, I'll try for sound waves. Those are pressure

waves or movements in the air that aren't always audible
to the human ear," she hastened to explain as Gram raised
a worried brow. "There are other tests I'd like to try later,
depending on the data I collect from these."

"When you're through with all those contraptions,
maybe that grandson of mine will see it's not my imagination that's been workin' late these past months. Christopher can be a stubborn man, and that's a fact."

Athena resisted adding her own pointed agreement to
this appraisal. Instead she decided somewhat shame-
facedly to take advantage of the comfortable atmosphere
between them to learn more about her enigmatic host.

"Christopher seems very interested in Scottish clans,"
she threw out casually. "That's a beautiful old book you
have in the library."

"It belonged to my late husband's grandfather, Sir
Henry Burke. Aye, and a very important man Sir Henry
was, too. The Burkes were major landowners in those
days, lassie. My, yes. Owned a good part of the countryside they did. And headed the clan, too. Burke House is
still the clan seat, you know."

Athena looked surprised. "No, I didn't know. Then
Christopher is the present head of Clan Burke."

"He is indeed, lass. And he takes the job seriously. 'Tis
me husband, his grandfather, he takes after. Our own son,
Christopher's late father, showed little interest in such
things. Too buried in his work he was, especially after
Mary, the wee bairns' mother, left." Gram sighed. "Aye,
that was a sad day."

Athena's attention was piqued by the mention of
Christopher's mother, but when the old woman showed no
inclination to pursue the tale, she reluctantly let it pass.

"Christopher has a brother, doesn't he?" she asked,
finishing the last of her soup.

"Aye, Ryan. Two years younger than Christopher, he is." A look of pride crossed the old woman's face, followed almost instantly by one of regret. "A bonny lad, our Ryan—too bonny by half, if the truth be known. A regular little rapscallion." Gram chuckled fondly. "Always gettin' himself into mischief."

Athena waited hopefully, but again the old woman showed no inclination to go on. Instead she stared out the window at the falling snow, seemingly lost in a past that only she could see.

"And Christopher?" Athena prodded gently. "Did he get into mischief, too?"

Gram snorted. "That lad? Never. Many's the time I wished he had. And he was even worse after Mary left." She shook her white head. "His mother's leavin' was a heavy blow, no doubt about it. But Ryan came out of it smartly enough. I always hoped Christopher would, too. Aye," she went on with a sigh, "Christopher's a good lad, but he's in sore need of more gaiety in his life, if you take my meanin'."

Athena not only "took" it, she heartily agreed, remembering that she'd yet to see the man smile. Without thinking, she blurted, "Doesn't he go out? I mean socially—with women?"

Now why in the world had she asked that? Feeling her cheeks flush, Athena hid her embarrassment by taking a bite of sandwich.

Gram apparently saw nothing wrong with Athena's curiosity. "Not since Sylvia," she said shortly, and Athena was surprised by the old woman's rancor. "And it's sorry he'll be one day. Aye, mark my words, lassie. Christopher will rue the day he let love for a woman close him off like that."

Gram's words haunted Athena throughout the remainder of the afternoon. Who was Sylvia? she wondered. Was this the elusive wife who had disppeared ten years ago? What had happened to her? Was she still alive? Again Athena wished that the old woman had been more specific. Her vague remarks had merely increased Athena's curiosity, not satisfied it. The master of Burke House remained as maddeningly mysterious as ever.

Christopher did not come home until almost dark, and judging by the snow still clinging to his suit and shoes, Athena deduced that even the Land Rover had experienced difficulties making it through the unabating storm.

She was taking another set of preliminary readings from the instruments outside Gram's room when he came upstairs. He looked tired, she thought, and a bit out of sorts. Perhaps being stuck inside the castle hadn't been so terrible after all, she decided, watching him brush snow from his hair. At least she'd gotten better acquainted with Gram and made a good start on her investigation.

"You've been busy I see," he said a little shortly, glancing at Athena's assortment of instruments. "I didn't realize ghost hunting had become such a science."

"You'd be surprised what we can do now," she said, keeping her voice friendly.

"And your, ah, tingles and goose bumps?"

She smiled. "Still tell me there's something here."

"I see." He reached for the handle to his grandmother's door. "And which will you believe if your instruments indicate that your instincts are wrong?"

"I have faith in my instincts," she told him evenly. "Frankly I'll be very surprised if the readings are totally negative."

"If I didn't know better, I'd say I detect a note of bias in that," he said, his tone faintly scornful.

"When it comes time to interpret the data I'll be strictly objective," she told him. "I never allow personal feelings to intrude on my work."

His expression was speculative as he opened his grandmother's door. "Don't you, Athena? I wonder."

That night Gram joined them downstairs for dinner. A smiling Fiona and a less-dour-than-usual Lachlan waited upon the old woman as if she was visiting royalty. Through it all, Gram beamed like a delighted child.

"They may be feedin' me the same food up there," she said, nodding toward the stairs, "but it surely tastes better down here!" She squinted across the table at Athena. "Are you goin' to keep fiddlin' with those gadgets of yours tonight, then?"

Athena caught Christopher's warning glance. "I'd like to, yes," she said, avoiding his look. "If it won't bother you."

"Och! Doin' somethin' about that rascal MacKay is not apt to be botherin' me, lass. You can read those whachamacallits all night long if it helps get rid of him."

"Athena can work just as well during the day," Christopher broke in with quiet firmness. "From what I've seen, she's already been at it long enough. She must be tired."

Athena knew his words were meant as much as a warning to her as an excuse to his grandmother. It might be his house, but she found his interference in her work galling. Gram's fears had to be considered first, as well as the success of her investigation. Since the apparition seemed far more likely to manifest itself at night, setting up outside the old woman's room would suit her purposes perfectly. Ignoring Christopher, she said, "I think it would be a good idea if I kept watch."

"I'm sure that won't be necessary." This time there was an unmistakable edge to his voice. "My grandmother has had an unusually busy day. If she's not disturbed I'm sure she'll sleep quite soundly tonight."

Hours later, Athena restlessly paced her room, cursing Christopher Burke and envying anyone who was currently enjoying some sleep in that cold, drafty house.

"Blast the man!" she exploded, thinking again of the infuriating little scenario he'd played out earlier. After calmly overriding Athena, he'd politely excused himself from the dinner table, seen his grandmother to her room and simply disappeared—no explanations, no good-nights. After stewing impatiently in the library waiting for his return, Athena had finally been forced to accept the fact that he was not coming back downstairs. For an hour or so she'd tried to make some use of the evening by reading, then, finding herself unable to concentrate, she'd gathered up several books on Scottish history and trudged upstairs to pace and brood about mule-headed, cantankerous Scotsmen!

What kind of game was he playing with her? she fumed. What good did it do to set up her equipment if she couldn't be on hand to take the readings? Gram's ghost was a night walker. She could sit outside the old woman's room for the entire day, but if the apparition didn't make an appearance all the instruments in the world wouldn't solve the mystery. She had to have the freedom to conduct the investigation in her own way. If Christopher was going to tie her hands, she might just as well pack up and leave.

Hearing one of the clocks in the hall strike eleven, Athena reached a decision. After all, what did she have to lose by going against his wishes? He might order her out of the castle, yet staying on like this was not only frustrating, it was a complete waste of time. At this rate, the ghost of

Angus MacKay would still be stalking Burke House for another 350 years!

Resolutely Athena pulled on her coat and tugged a ski cap over her mop of curls. Gathering up her infrared camera and flashlight, she slipped quietly out of her room and down the stairs to the first landing.

The house was eerily still. Stopping in front of Gram's door, Athena pressed her ear against the heavy wood panel and listened. Inside, she could hear the old woman snoring softly; she was fast asleep.

Good, Athena thought, scanning the hallway for the best vantage point. Choosing a position across the corridor from the old woman's room, she pulled over a hall chair and set up her camera. Next she carefully examined each of her instruments and turned on the polygraphs.

Now for the lights. Very quietly, she made her way down the length of the corridor, switching off each of the small, old-fashioned wall sconces that lined either side of the hallway. She wanted it as dark as possible, both to hide her own presence and to help eliminate the possibility of fraud. If someone was playing a cruel sort of joke on Gram, Athena planned to be in position to expose the deception. With the aid of her infrared camera, capable of taking pictures in total darkness, she'd be ideally situated. If Gram's apparition "walked" tonight, she'd be ready for it.

She did not have long to wait. Shortly before midnight Athena sensed that something was about to happen. The familiar prickles started at the base of her neck, and she had a strong feeling she was no longer alone.

Oh-oh, she thought, clenching her camera a little tighter. Here it comes. Straining to see through the darkness, she thought she could make out a vague luminescence at the end of the hallway. Realizing how easy it was to imagine things under these circumstances, Athena closed her eyes tightly, then slowly opened them again. Her pulse jumped and she sucked in her breath. There it was, even brighter now. She hadn't imagined it!

Trying to hold in her excitement, Athena examined the apparition. It was a shapeless, luminous veil of white light, bright in the center and becoming gradually blurred about the edges. Although it appeared to be floating along several inches off the floor, Athena thought she could make out the very faint sound of footsteps. Silently she watched it draw closer. It was moving in a straight line toward Gram's door!

Very, very quietly, Athena raised the camera and aimed it at the glowing object, pressing her finger down on the shutter when she was sure she had it in her sights. She held her breath as the soft whirr of the advancing film cut through the deathly silence of the castle. Would the noise frighten it away? she thought anxiously. Would it sense her hiding there in the darkness and disappear?

Suddenly Athena felt a terrible chill. Shivering, she stopped taking pictures for a moment to pull her coat collar up around her neck. Without thinking, she turned to see if someone had left a window open, then remembered there were no windows in that part of the corridor. Nor were there any doors leading to the outside at this level of the castle. She felt her flesh tingle as she realized there was no physical explanation for the sudden chill. Unless she was very mistaken it was part of the light. She had to stop herself from exclaiming out loud in her excitement. If her instruments validated what she was picking up visually, she was really on to something!

Even as her heart thudded in anticipation, her fingers automatically went back to the camera, snapping pictures furiously. It was almost upon her—the light seemed to fill

the hall with an unnatural brilliance. Then, when she felt
as if she might reach out and touch it, a door suddenly
slammed behind her and the sound reverberated violently
through the quiet hallway. Athena's taut nerves snapped
at the unexpected noise, and she cursed beneath her breath
as the camera toppled from her grasp. By the time she'd
retrieved it, the corridor was once again in total darkness.
As if it had been turned off by a phantom switch, the luminous light had vanished.

"Ouch!" There was a loud scuffle behind her, followed
by a crash and an unmistakable voice demanding, "What
the hell is going on out here?"

Athena's heart sank. Christopher! "Wait a minute," she
called out softly. "I've got a light."

Athena placed the camera on the chair, then felt about
on the floor for the flashlight. In a few seconds the beam
picked out Christopher's angry face glaring at her through
the darkness. He was standing by a heavy oak table just
past the turn in the landing, the broken remains of a Vic-
torian vase lying at his feet.

"Are you all right?" she asked, watching guiltily as he
bent to massage his foot. "I guess you must have banged
against the table in the dark."

"How perceptive of you," he replied dryly. "What in
hell has happened to all the lights?"

"I turned them off." Athena turned the beam to the
closest light fixture. "Wait. I'll have them on again in a
minute." She went from one wall sconce to the next
switching on the lights. When the corridor was once again
filled with soft illumination, she turned back to find him
regarding her angrily.

"I thought I told you to stay in your room," he said in
a loud whisper. "It's bad enough that you upset my

grandmother with this foolishness during the day. I won't have you disturbing her sleep, as well."

"The only one who seems to be disturbed is you," she said, motioning him to be quiet. "And you're making enough noise about it." She went over and placed her ear quietly on Gram's door, relieved to hear the steady rumble of soft snoring inside. "Fortunately she's hard of hearing and slept through all that clamor you made."

"All the clamor *I* made!" He opened his mouth, then closed it, glaring at her instead. "I think it's time we had a talk." Stalking over, he took her firmly by the wrist.

"Where are we going?" Athena asked, startled as he pulled her along behind him, across the top of the landing and down the opposite hallway. Outmatched by his longer strides, she had to run to keep up with him. "Let me go, will you? I can walk by myself."

His only answer was to slow down the pace sufficiently so that she could keep up. Stopping midway down the hall, he threw open a door. "In here," he said, nudging her none too gently inside.

Before she could protest, he'd switched on the light and led her over to a chair. "Sit," he ordered.

Doing as she was told, Athena took a moment to catch her breath and to take stock of her surroundings. Compared to the other rooms she'd seen at Burke House, this one was relatively small. It appeared more lived in than the others, almost cozy.

While Christopher turned his back to stoke the fire, she noted that the most dominant piece of furniture in the room was a desk, its top stacked with an orderly confusion of papers and files. To one side was a coffee mug, to the other a framed picture of Gram. The wall to the right of the desk held a bookcase and typewriter, the one opposite it a large color map of Scotland. Featured over the fireplace was the Clan Burke crest, with the familiar lion and horse holding up the ancient family shield.

The room was a place to work, she decided. More than that, she suspected it was a place to get away. A thin film of dust on one of the bookcases told her it was a hideaway safe from dusting, prying or rearranging hands. Christopher would come here to think, and perhaps to escape, she thought. It was a very male refuge, a warrior's lair.

Some of his anger had abated by the time he finished with the fireplace. It seemed to have been replaced by a sharp wariness. He kept his eyes on her as he sat down behind the desk. "It's almost one o'clock in the morning," he informed her unnecessarily. "Why aren't you in bed?"

"Because I had work to do."

"Playing with your little gadgets."

"I was attempting to take some scientific readings," she corrected angrily.

"Scientific." He spat the word out scornfully. Then his eyes hardened. "Who are you trying to fool with this psychic nonsense? Don't you think it's time we discussed what you're really up to?"

Athena looked at him in honest surprise. "What do you mean, what I'm up to? You know very well why I came here."

"I know the reason you gave. It's the truth we're talking about now."

She looked at him for a moment, trying to read his expression. "You're serious, aren't you?" she said in slow amazement. She stood and moved to the bookcase. Folding her arms across her chest, she stared at him. "All right, Christopher, this is your party. You're the one doing all the guessing. Tell me, why am I supposed to have come to Burke House?"

He made a short, disgusted sound. "I'm getting tired of the games, Athena. We both know how long your father's clan has been trying to get Kildrurry. Over the years they've attempted everything from hard-luck stories to threatened lawsuits to achieve their ends. What happened? Did the MacKays finally exhaust their little bag of tricks? Is that why they sent you?"

"The MacKay clan doesn't even know I'm here. I came because my father asked me to." Athena felt the familiar choke of anguish in her chest when she remembered the last scene with her dad. Sometimes she wondered if she would ever get used to his being gone.

"And what were your orders? To insinuate your way into my grandmother's confidence? Or perhaps mine?" Something hard had entered his voice, an edge of bitterness. "You're a beautiful woman, Athena. Was that the plan? If the MacKays couldn't get Kildrurry by more conventional means, they wouldn't hesitate to resort to sex?"

Athena gasped. "Sex! You think I came here to *seduce* you?"

"I think you came prepared to do whatever it takes to get back Kildrurry."

She was staring at him incredulously. "Including luring you to bed."

He leaned back in his chair. "If all else failed."

For a moment Athena was too shocked to protest. Then fury overcame disbelief. "Why you—you bastard! How dare you?"

He eyed her coolly. "It's late, Athena. Surely you're not going to waste my time and yours by denying you came to Scotland to reclaim Kildrurry."

"I'm not going to deny a damn thing," she spat. "An accusation like that doesn't deserve a denial. It's too ludicrous."

He shrugged and rose. "Then it appears we have a stalemate."

"Only because you're too stubborn to listen to the truth. Everything my father said about the Burkes was right. It may be three hundred years, but some things just don't change."

His voice remained maddeningly calm. "You're telling me you didn't come here to press the MacKay claim!?"

"Of course I did. But not that way. Never *that* way!"

"Of course not."

Athena wanted to slap the smug look off his face. "Damn you, don't be condescending with me. What makes you think I'd even want to go to bed with you? You place a pretty high value on yourself to suppose I'd travel halfway around the world to make love to an overbearing, arrogant, self-centered mercenary!"

"Watch out, Athena," he said with deceptive quiet. "You're hardly in a position to be name calling."

"No, I forgot," she blazed. "I'm here to seduce you to achieve my foul ends." She paced angrily to the bookcase, then turned to him. "And would it have worked? If I'd lured you to bed, would you have given us back Kildrurry?"

Something new flickered in his cool eyes, then was gone. "Don't be ridiculous."

"Ridiculous?" The word choked in her throat. "You have the gall to call *me* ridiculous?" She ignored the warning glint in his eyes. She didn't see the tight, thin set of his mouth. She wanted to taunt him, she wanted to make him angry, she wanted him to lose that granite control. "What's the matter, Christopher?" she goaded. "Don't I appeal to you? Aren't I sexy enough for you?"

His eyes gleamed dangerously in the firelight. "Drop it, Athena."

"Oh, but I'm curious," she went on sweetly. "The MacKays would be disappointed to find that they'd sent me all this way on a wild-goose chase."

"It's late," he said tightly. "We'll continue this discussion tomorrow."

She smiled at him and moved fractionally closer, allowing her arm to brush against his. "No, we'll discuss it tonight. You've set me wondering. Maybe I don't turn you on. Is that it, Christopher?"

He caught her scent and something in him reacted to the soft touch of her skin. She was deliberately baiting him. She wanted him to react. But though he knew exactly what she was doing, he couldn't stop the sharp stirring of his body.

"What are you trying to do, Athena?" he asked tightly as she ran a finger along the side of his face.

Her hazel eyes flew open innocently. "Why I'm trying my damnedest to seduce you, Christopher. Isn't that what you expected me to do?"

When her fingers reached the hollow of his neck, he grabbed her upper arms to keep them still. "I expected you to have better sense than to try a crazy stunt like this."

She pouted up at him seductively. "Oh, and here I thought I was doing so well." His show of force merely retriggered her anger. Was brute strength the only way he knew to deal with a situation? "What's the matter, Christopher?" she purred. "Are you afraid of me? Are you afraid you can't handle a real woman?"

Christopher gave her shoulders a shake. "Dammit, Athena. Don't you know you're playing with fire?"

"My, my. So the big, tough man has emotions after all. For a while there I thought I might be dealing with a sphinx."

The air exploded out of her lungs as he suddenly crushed her into his chest. She couldn't speak—she could barely breathe. She looked up into his dark face and saw cold fury, and for the first time considered what she might have unleashed. "Is that what you want, Athena? Do you really want to see me lose control?"

"You can let me go now," she snapped, trying not to let him sense her fear. "Once again you've proved your superior strength. I'm suitably impressed. Now let me go!"

Athena felt as if she were caught in a steel clamp. Looking up into the icy hardness of his eyes, her fear turned to anger. How dare he flaunt his masculinity like this! How typical of a Burke—take possession by any means or method available. Using the only weapon she had left, she lashed out at him with her tongue. "Is this how you get your kicks, Christopher? By showing how powerful you are? Does it make you feel like a real he-man to ride roughshod over someone who's weaker than you?"

"For God's sake, woman," he rasped. "Hold your tongue."

She had only enough time to register the gleaming fury in his eyes and to curse herself soundly for pushing him too far. Then it was too late. Powerless to move, Athena waited helplessly while his mouth swooped down to possess hers.

Five

There was something almost savage about the way his lips claimed hers. His fury was evident in the primitive way he forced apart her lips and took total possession of her mouth. He was attempting to control her, to dominate her in the most fundamental male sense. There was a raw desperation in his actions, as if he were determined to vent the full depth of his anger and frustration in this one kiss.

Athena couldn't breathe. She couldn't move. Her body strained against the power of his grip, but there was no give in the steel embrace that held her captive. From somewhere she heard the sound of an impatient groan, and blood seemed to pound in her ears. The room was spinning crazily. Athena felt desperate to stay afloat, and so she was forced to hold on to him even as she fought fruitlessly to pull away.

Then, as suddenly as the assault began, it stopped. Raising his head, Christopher gazed down at her, his breathing labored, his face strained. "Athena," he breathed. "What are you doing to me?"

Athena stood very still, too shaken to speak, not daring to move. She could see that his anger was receding, replaced by an expression she couldn't read. He stood there quietly studying her face as if he was seeing it for the first time. Gently he traced a thumb along the line of her hair, touching the curls that had come loose from her ski cap to rest softly next to her face.

With a sudden movement, he swept the cap to the floor, allowing the rich cascade of chestnut curls to fall to her shoulders. "You have lovely hair," he murmured, running his fingers through the luxurious, thick mass. "I love the way it catches the reds and golds of the fire. And your eyes—just when I think I know what color they are, they've changed on me again." His voice was husky, caressing. "God help me, Athena. You're so lovely!"

Then his mouth was on hers again, but this time it was a gentle, tender pressure. His tongue probed the line of her lips, seeking permission to enter. Where he had earlier laid brutal claim, he now sought, he requested.

Athena's senses were whirling at the sudden change in his lovemaking. She had the peculiar sensation of being suspended in time, and the drugging kiss was dulling her perceptions. She realized that this time he was giving of himself as well as taking from her. The hunger was still there, but it was now controlled, it was subservient to his desire to bring her pleasure. Athena trembled at the wonderful ache knotting deep in her body. She had goaded him, accused him of being unable to respond emotionally to a woman. But oh, she'd been wrong. There was a world of emotion in his embrace, and heaven help her, she was being swept up into the very vortex of his passion.

Athena was bombarded by a dozen confused sensations—the tangy scent of his after-shave, the pounding thud of his heart against her breast, the pressure of his strong fingers still holding her but no longer hurting. All of them told her she wanted him. Never mind the wisdom or the prudence of it; any doubts she pushed aside. She wanted only to luxuriate in the feel of him, his warmth, his strength.

Eagerly she parted her lips, welcoming his kiss. Her mind was a whirling cloud of desire as she returned passion for passion, need for need. Losing sight of reality, she reveled in the heightening tension the kiss was generating inside her. She wanted only to quell the sweet, agonizing ache, to extinguish the fire he had started.

When Christopher felt the willing softening of her body, he broke the contact between them to murmur dazedly against her mouth, "Athena, do you have any idea what you're doing to me?"

Athena looked up at him, but she was too dazed to speak. Then his lips were back, and she felt her body pressed persuasively into his. Tongue met tongue as he sought to discover the sweet hidden mysteries of her mouth. She melted beneath the dizzying onslaught, clinging to his powerful shoulders for support, returning pleasure for pleasure, matching his passion.

Her invitation acted like a torch to dry kindling. Moaning softly, Christopher set about the deliberate invasion of her senses. His fingers brushed lightly against the curved fullness of her breasts, stroking them easily, delighting in the answering thrust of her nipples. One hand slid down the slender line of her back to arch her against him and she gasped softly when she realized just how intensely he was able to respond to a woman.

Even more surprising was her own reaction. Trembling with the force of her excitement and growing need, her nails bit into the skin of his shoulders, her eager moan matching the burgeoning ache of her body. She thrilled to the hard, taut contours of him, to the way he was breathing her name into her hair.

Very gently he cupped her face in his hands and looked down into the warm, amber depths of her eyes. Then, bending his head, he held her still as he rained a fiery line of kisses across her cheeks and down the graceful curve of her neck. He felt her shiver as his hands slipped lower to trace the line of her shoulders, then lower still to the soft swell of her breasts.

The heat in her seemed to radiate out and envelop him. Her cheeks were flushed, her eyes half-closed and dazed with desire. Her responses fired him to new levels of passion. Never before had he wanted a woman like this. He ached to take her here and now, to lower himself into her warm, moist softness. He knew that his ability to stop was very nearly gone. How easy it would be to let himself go, to claim what he knew could be his for the asking. No matter that this was what she wanted, what she had planned from the beginning.

The passion surging through him didn't want to abate. He fought back the waves of desire, willing control, sanity, to return. He held her very still, trying not to feel the soft thrust of her body against his. His breathing was labored from the effort it was costing him, and when he finally spoke, the terse, clipped words were forced through clenched teeth.

"I think we've gone far enough. You nearly won, didn't you, Athena? You play the game very well."

For a minute she couldn't understand what he was saying, then the full realization of his meaning hit her like a

splash of ice water. Shaking with fury, she wrenched herself from his grasp, staring up at him in shocked disbelief.
"Why you—you overweening, egotistical bastard!"

"You've already called me that once tonight," he said,
moving to put some distance between them. He could still
taste her, feel her softness. Damn the woman, he still
wanted her!

"A dozen times wouldn't be enough," she shot at him
heatedly. "How can you accuse me of setting this up? You
initiated it, remember?"

"After you went out of your way to provoke me."

"What was I supposed to do when you accused me of
being a—a Jezebel!"

"A name you've done your best to live up to. For all
your protesting, you certainly know how to get to a man."

She glared at him, experiencing a hurt so intense she felt
sick. It was true, she'd wanted him, she'd responded to him
fully, knowing the logical course their lovemaking would
take. And he'd used her—toyed with her to see how far she
would go. Athena felt ashamed and betrayed. In her humiliation, she hid behind a very real wall of fury.

"I suppose I ought to congratulate myself then," she
mocked, each word a scathing accusation. "Getting some
kind of human response out of you is a real accomplish-
ment—a minor miracle!"

She saw quick anger across his face, and then it was
gone. "It's nearly 2:00 A.M.," he said quietly. "If you're
through I'd like to get some sleep tonight."

"No, I'm not through. I want to know where I stand.
You've accused me of coming here under false pretenses.
Does that mean you want me to leave?"

He hesitated. "There are complications that have to be
considered."

"You mean Gram."

He felt another flash of anger. "For one thing."

"And what else? There's another reason, isn't there?"

Something in his face made her guess the answer. "You want me to fail, don't you? Of course, that would solve all your problems very neatly. Not only would Gram be convinced that old Angus is a figment of her imagination, but it would effectively shut up the MacKays."

"I'm beginning to think that's an impossibility," he told her dryly.

"Why? Because we care enough to fight for what's rightfully ours?"

"Because you're too bloody stubborn to admit it's not. The MacKays lost Kildrurry over three hundred years ago. Why can't you people accept that fact and let go of it?"

"Some things are important enough to hang on to," she told him. "Some injustices take longer than others to set right."

"And that's what you plan to do, Athena? Set everything right?"

His condescending look was infuriating. "I plan to give it a damn good try. And not, I might add, by luring you to bed."

"By using all those devices you've set up in the hall, then? I thought we had disposed of this psychic nonsense."

She took a deep mental breath. "You've already made your views on the subject abundantly clear," she said evenly. "I simply want to know if I'm to be allowed to finish my work here."

"Searching for a ghost."

"Doing whatever it takes to help Gram," she retorted angrily. "I know you won't believe this, but there *is* something out there. I saw it myself—tonight."

"You saw it." For a moment she thought he was going to laugh. "And what does it look like, Athena? Does it wear a sheet? Is it dragging chains?"

Athena closed her eyes in hopeless frustration. Reasoning with him was useless. It was time to play her ace, to take advantage of the one chink she'd found in the Viking's armor.

"There's no sense going around about this," she said, ignoring his baiting. "If you want me to leave just say so, and I'll be out of here the moment the storm breaks. But you'll have to be the one to tell your grandmother. I've given her my word. I want her to understand why I'm being forced to break it."

He was silent for a long moment, and Athena found herself holding her breath. Christopher knew his grandmother was upset. He might not accept the possibility of a ghost, but he couldn't ignore her fears. And he loved her; that was the one constant Athena had to fall back on. Would he risk the setback it might mean to Gram's health if she was to leave?

He was watching her with a quiet, calculating expression. "If," he began cautiously, "I were to give you time to complete your work here, would you be willing to promise me, on behalf of the entire MacKay clan, to bury the subject of Kildrurry and Angus MacKay?"

"I have no authority to make a promise like that. I told you, I'm not here as a clan representative."

"So you've said. But as your father's daughter, your word must carry some weight. If you go back and tell them you've failed to find one shred of evidence to support the MacKay claim, they'll have to listen to you."

"I suppose," Athena agreed, knowing it was true. Her father had said it and the clan would have to accept it. She was their last hope.

He was watching her closely. "Then you accept these conditions?"

Realizing she had no choice, Athena slowly nodded. "How long will you give me?"

"Three weeks. That's the date we plan to break ground for the Kildrurry Golf Course. If you've been unable to help my grandmother by then, or failed to find your *proof* for the MacKays, then I want the entire subject closed, once and for all." Again his eyes held her captive. "Do you understand, Athena? At the end of that time I never want to hear about this Angus MacKay business again—no letters, no threatened lawsuits, nothing."

"I understand." Three weeks. Would it be enough time? She'd have to *make* it be enough. "During that time you agree to allow me the freedom to conduct my investigation in my own way?"

He hesitated a moment. "Within limits."

"No limits," she interjected quickly. "You can't bind my hands."

Reluctantly he nodded. "All right. But my grandmother must not be harmed—in any way. Deal or no deal, that has to be the primary consideration."

"I don't want to see her hurt, either. Believe me, that's the last thing I want to see happen!"

Athena went down to breakfast early the next morning. It had finally stopped snowing, but there was still no possibility of driving out. Fiona seemed hopeful that by afternoon the sun would warm sufficiently to melt most of the drifts. In the meantime they all continued to be stuck.

Including Christopher. She passed him in the entry hall on her way into the dining room. After looking momentarily surprised to see her up and about so early, he wished her a polite good-morning.

"I see even you couldn't make it out today," she replied, matching his reserve. So that was the way it was going to be for the next three weeks, she thought. Courteous coexistence. Well, so be it. Remembering last night's scene with him in the study, she decided it could be a good deal worse.

"No, although I expect they'll have the roads cleared by later this afternoon," he told her. "Until then, I'll be working at home."

Although she didn't see Christopher again for the remainder of the morning, Athena was painfully aware of his presence in the house. Every time the floor creaked or a door was closed, she found she was looking over her shoulder to see if it was him.

"Dad, if it wasn't for you I'd leave," she muttered, hating the feeling of losing control over her life. "You and Gram. Too many promises," she told the polygraph machine as she changed a roll of paper. "I've got to stop making promises!"

After she had attended to her instruments, Athena gathered up last night's roll of exposed film and set out to find a suitable place to develop it. A seldom-used bathroom was her best bet, she thought. One located where she wouldn't be interrupted at the wrong moment.

She found what she was looking for at the end of her own corridor. The sink was a bit more old-fashioned than she would have liked, but it was situated between two bedrooms that weren't in use, and that would be to her advantage.

Hauling her developing equipment into the makeshift darkroom, she cleared off the top of a cabinet and set up her supplies. After replacing the light bulb with one of her own, she was ready to begin.

The first few photographs were much as she expected, a clear view of the empty hallway outside Gram's room facing north. They would serve nicely as control shots, she thought, to show how the deserted corridor normally looked late at night.

Her pulse rate increased markedly when she set about developing the next set of pictures. There, very faintly, she could make out a vague light in the center of the hallway, looking little more than a shapeless fog. In subsequent pictures, the light became increasingly brighter and more focused. There was still no distinct shape, but the varying degrees of light were more apparent. It was as if the fog were lit from within, from an inner, luminescent core.

"That's it," she said aloud, taking the photos out of the solution of sodium thiosulfate. "As hard evidence, they're inconclusive. But taken along with the instrument readings, they show that *something* is out there!"

Carefully Athena developed the rest of the roll, cringing slightly as the last few pictures came out of the hypo. They were of Christopher, a very surprised, very angry Christopher caught in the act of hitting his shin on the leg of the table. Seeing him there reminded her of the scene that followed between them in his study, and she was once again caught between humiliation and fury.

How dare he, she thought, jerking the prints more roughly than necessary through the solutions. What colossal nerve to think she'd willingly use her body to achieve her ends.

But you would have let him make love to you, came the persistent voice of truth. You were ready—anxious for him to take you!

With a muttered oath, Athena yanked the remaining prints out of the pan. This just proved how insidiously this house was getting to her. She had to complete her work and get out of there. The sooner the better!

On her way to have tea with Gram that afternoon, Athena discovered the roads had been cleared and, true to Fiona's prediction, much of the snow had melted. Now that it was possible to drive in and out again, the old woman announced they would be having guests for dinner.

"William and Megan Begley," Clara told her excitedly. "William is Christopher's right-hand man in the business." She chuckled, obviously looking forward to the party with childlike anticipation. "Those lads practically grew up together."

"And Megan. That's Mr. Begley's wife?"

"No, no, Megan is his sister. And bonnie she is, too." Gram leaned forward, grinning. "She designs dresses—you know, the fancy ones you see in all the magazines. Aye," she concluded, nodding her head knowingly. "There's no doubt that Megan Begley is a very clever lass."

When the guests arrived shortly before seven that evening, Athena was struck by the inadequacy of Gram's description. To say that Megan Begley was "bonnie," would be like calling Michelangelo's *David* cute.

In her early thirties, the woman was dressed in a knee-length creation of russet silk crepe de chine that cleverly matched her flowing mane of copper-colored hair. An inch or two taller than Athena's five-foot-eight, Megan had both the figure and the carriage of a professional model. Her hands were slender and very graceful, her nails long and polished to match her dress. Quite simply, Megan Begley was a knockout and, to Athena's unaccountable dismay, on extremely friendly terms with Christopher.

Hold on, Athena, she warned herself abruptly. It's no business of yours if he has a dozen Megan Begleys tucked away somewhere. Adjourning to the library for before-dinner cocktails, Athena sat a bit apart from the others and, trying to ignore the familiar repartee between Christopher and Megan, she turned her attention to the woman's brother.

He was tall and had the same flame-colored hair as his sister. Like Christopher, he was expensively turned out in a dark, tailor-made suit. In William's case, however, he wore the clothes almost indifferently, as if he would have been equally comfortable in jeans and a T-shirt. He had a happy-go-lucky air about him that Athena took to immediately. Like her father, William Begley was Athena's idea of an amicable Scotsman—loud, good-natured and full of outlandish anecdotes.

She hoped she might be seated next to William at dinner, but found herself instead with Megan as a dining companion. Knowing it was petty and unfair, she nonetheless expected Megan to be as aloof as she was beautiful. It came as a pleasant surprise to find that she was just the opposite.

"I'm so glad to meet you at last," Megan told her with genuine warmth. "When Christopher told me that a parapsychologist was staying at Burke House, I must admit I didn't expect anyone like you."

Athena held up a hand. "Don't tell me. You pictured a gypsy carrying a crystal ball."

"And two or three spirit trumpets." She leaned over and spoke confidentially. "I'm fascinated by the supernatural. Christopher thinks it's all nonsense, of course, but I confess that I find it exciting. Tell me, have you seen the infamous Angus yet?"

Much to her surprise, Athena found herself sharing what she had uncovered so far in her investigation, including the ghostly light in the corridor. She laughed when

Megan shivered delightedly and claimed she'd give up several fashion commissions to have a peek at the "old boy."

"Who knows," Athena told her, "perhaps it can be arranged." She stole a surreptitious glance at the head of the table. That ought to give Christopher apoplexy, she thought.

As if reading her thoughts, Megan waved her hand dismissively. "I'm not sure Christopher would admit to a ghost even if it were to come up to him and introduce itself. Secretly, though, I suspect he takes a certain pride in having a resident *ghaistie*. All the best Scottish castles have them, you know."

After dinner Gram retired, weary but satisfied, to her room. Throughout the meal she'd been in her glory, sitting opposite her grandson and enjoying her role as grande dame to the hilt.

Athena was seriously considering joining the older woman, when Christopher announced his intentions of discussing some business matters with William in the study. Not wanting to leave Megan alone, Athena accompanied her to the library. As usual, Lachlan brought in a tray of coffee, then stoked the fire and executed his customary silent retreat.

"I can't get over how much better Gram looks," Megan told her, settling comfortably in her chair. "You're exactly what the doctor ordered. This house has been getting entirely too depressive lately."

"She's a wonderful lady," Athena said fondly. "Considering her age and the state of her health, she's remarkably feisty."

"She's had to be. Over the years Clara Burke has had her share of problems. She's a survivor." Megan sipped her coffee, then looked at Athena as if reaching a decision. "I think you're just what Christopher needs, too."

Athena looked at her in surprise. "But I thought that you and he—"

"Were romantically involved?" She laughed. "No, although my mother tried her best to push us in that direction. It wasn't meant to be, I'm afraid. William and Christopher grew up together and I was always the tagalong, the little sister. Much as I love him, Christopher will always be just another big brother."

"Oh." Athena refused to acknowledge an unbidden surge of relief. It's no concern of yours, she reminded herself sharply. "Then you knew Christopher's brother, Ryan," she asked, steering her mind in a safer direction.

A shadow crossed Megan's lovely face. "How much has he told you about his family?"

Athena shook her head and answered honestly. "Very little."

Megan finished her coffee, then put the cup on the table. For a moment she gazed into the fire. Her expression was pensive, Athena thought, much as Christopher's had been the night he'd sat in the same seat and debated whether to tell her the story of Angus MacKay. They were both hiding something, she realized. What?

Megan looked away from the fire and fixed Athena with a penetrating look. "You're interested in Christopher, aren't you?"

"He..." Athena hesitated, not knowing how to answer. "He's a fascinating man. Of course I'm interested."

"No. I meant more than that." Megan thought of the private, sidelong looks Christopher and Athena had given each other at dinner, of the electricity that flowed almost palpably between the two. She decided to be blunt. "You care for him in a personal way, don't you?"

Athena couldn't answer. She wanted to smile and deny that her feelings for Christopher were in any way personal. They were as different as night and day; they had nothing in common. There was no reason for her to care. Instead she found herself nodding a silent yes.

Megan smiled. "I like you, Athena. And I meant what I said about your being good for this family. Because of that, well, I'm going to tell you more than I probably should. If Christopher found out he'd be upset with me. But I think you should know."

"Yes," Athena said softly. "I would like to know."

"Christopher never talks about it. Even then, when he was a small child, he tried to close it off."

"His mother?" Athena guessed.

Megan nodded. "It happened when Christopher was eight and his brother Ryan six. Their mother ran off with one of her husband's friends. Christopher's father was devastated. Needless to say, so were the boys. Ryan soon pulled out of it—he was the more outgoing of the two— and I suspect he might have even used his mother's absence and his father's growing preoccupation with his business to run a bit wilder than he might have otherwise.

"Christopher was different. I was only four at the time, but even then I sensed a change in him. He seemed to grow up overnight. Suddenly he was the responsible one, the child everyone could count on. His father was so rarely at home...." She shrugged sadly. "In many ways Christopher became the man of the house."

Athena thought sadly of the little boy forced too soon to become an adult—to become serious about life. And also to bury feelings that were too painful to acknowledge? she wondered. "And Gram raised them?"

"Yes, with a string of nursemaids who came and went over the years. Ryan was a handful. I gather it was difficult to keep anyone for very long."

"And—Christopher's wife?" Athena broached tentatively.

Megan sighed. "Christopher married shortly out of college. Sylvia, his wife, was young and very beautiful. He'd met her abroad, on a post-graduation ski trip to the Alps. When the vacation ended it became an explosive, long distance courtship. Sylvia was from Ireland, and of course by then Christopher had settled here and was working for his father."

"But they married."

"Yes, they married," Megan repeated quietly. "They had a whirlwind honeymoon—all over the Continent— anywhere and everywhere that took their fancy. When it was over, Sylvia couldn't seem to settle down. She was restless at Burke House. It was too old, too drafty, too far removed from the excitement of city life. She wanted to travel, to show off her beautiful clothes, to dine in fine restaurants, to, well, to live."

"And Christopher?" She tried to imagine him with his beautiful young bride. Had he smiled more then? Had he tried to please her, to make her more content? Somehow she had a difficult time thinking of him as being young and in love.

"I think Christopher realized his father wouldn't be around much longer," Megan told her. "He devoted himself to learning the business. I think he loved Sylvia, but I'm not sure he knew how to make her happy."

"And Ryan? I suppose he was still in school?"

Megan made an impatient little sound in her throat. "Ryan was always in one school or another—but rarely the same one for more than a few months at a time. He had difficulty following rules, the school's or anyone else's. When he wore out his welcome at one university, his father always managed to buy his way into another. Finally Ryan tired of the charade and came home. For a time he tried working for his father and brother, then, when George Burke died, Ryan took his share of the inheritance and bought into an export firm that promised him the kind of life he was looking for."

Megan paused, then went on quietly. "Sylvia went with him."

"Oh, my God! With Ryan?" Athena's eyes flew open in shock. "You mean just like that? With Christopher's brother?"

"Ostensibly Sylvia was going to Paris to shop. After two weeks a letter arrived announcing that she wasn't coming back. It was only then that Christopher discovered she'd closed her personal bank accounts and taken everything of value that would fit in her suitcases."

"He must have been furious. Crushed!"

"If he was he never let it show." She poured fresh coffee into their cups. "It was his father's story all over again. Christopher threw himself into his work. And when he wasn't building something or buying something or swinging some sort of a deal, he buried himself away here, with Gram."

"The one person in the world he knew he could count on," Athena murmured softly.

"That's about it."

Athena shook her head, trying to absorb it all. Of course he was bitter. Who wouldn't be bitter given the same circumstances? Deserted as a child by his mother. Deserted as an adult by his wife. No wonder he couldn't trust.

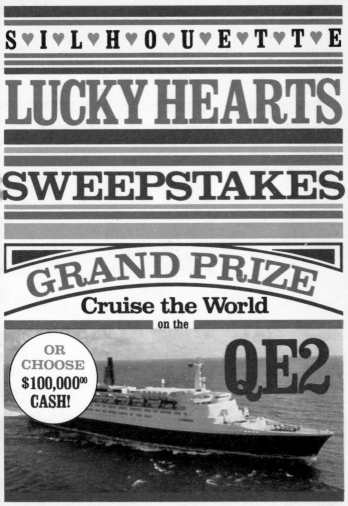

GET 4 FREE BOOKS, FREE FOLDING UMBRELLA, FREE MYSTERY GIFT!

TO ENTER: Fill out, detach below, and affix postage. See back pages of books for OFFICIAL SWEEPSTAKES INFORMATION and mail your entry before deadline date shown in rules.

OFFICIAL ENTRY/ORDER

Lucky Hearts Sweepstakes

MAIL TODAY!

Check one:

☐ YES, enter me in the Lucky Hearts Sweepstakes and send me 4 FREE SILHOUETTE DESIRE novels plus a FREE FOLDING UMBRELLA, and FREE Mystery Gift. Then send me 6 brand-new Silhouette Desire novels every month for my FREE inspection. Unless I say stop, bill me just $11.70 (a $13.50 value) with no shipping or handling charges. I may cancel anytime I wish and the 4 FREE BOOKS, UMBRELLA and Mystery Gift are mine to keep.

☐ NO, I do not want to receive the 4 FREE Silhouette books, FREE Folding Umbrella and FREE Mystery Gift. Please enter me in the sweepstakes.

Name_____
(please print)

Address_____
(apt.)

City_____

State_____ Zip_____

Terms and prices subject to change. Your enrollment is subject to acceptance by Silhouette Books.

SILHOUETTE DESIRE is a registered trademark.   CSD5D6

S♥I♥L♥H♥O♥U♥E♥T♥T♥E
LUCKY HEARTS
SWEEPSTAKES

Free prizes—you must enter to win. Detach here and mail today!

Sweeps entry—
process immediately!

Silhouette Books®

Prize Headquarters
120 Brighton Road
P.O. Box 5084
Clifton, NJ 07015-5084

She stood suddenly and went to stand in front of the fire. "I'm glad you told me," she said slowly. "It explains so much."

"Yes, I thought it might," Megan said thoughtfully. She was quiet for a long moment, eyeing the younger woman appraisingly. Then, because she liked what she saw she added impulsively, "Be patient with him, Athena. He needs time to learn to feel again. I think you're the one to teach him. I think you're the one to bring Christopher back to life."

Six

The sun glittered over the green countryside, reflecting the graceful swing of Christopher's hammer. He enjoyed the easy rhythm, the solid contact of metal against wood. When he was working at a site he could relax, his body became a hard, well-coordinated machine. It was basic—the smell of lumber and perspiration, the comfortable camaraderie of the men, the satisfaction of creating something with your hands. To Christopher it was an escape valve for the pressures of his other world.

This morning there was one more reason to blow off steam—Athena MacKay. He didn't like what she was doing to him. As a child he'd learned that to survive in a difficult and frequently unfair world, he had to keep his emotions tightly chained. The other night, Athena had come very close to breaking that chain. He did not intend to let it happen again.

The problem, he admitted, was that he had let down his guard. For the past ten years no woman had been allowed into his life unless specifically invited—and then only when he was certain there was no possibility of emotional attachment. Athena had slipped past his protective shield.

Christopher hammered the last nail into the two-by-four, then ran the back of his hand over his damp forehead. Anyone passing the site might have taken him for one of the workers. Tight jeans molded his lean hips and powerful thighs, and a hard hat rested on his head. If the passerby bothered to look twice, however, he would have seen that the golden-haired giant was treated with a subtle air of deference. Beneath the jeans and hard hat, he was still the boss. He would always remain slightly apart.

Perhaps that was a factor, too, Christopher thought. Choosing to remain slightly separate from the social mainstream, he'd become overconfident of his ability to remain untouched by it. He had forgotten what it was like to really want a woman, what it was like to have one get under his skin.

Christopher swore as he lifted another two-by-four into place, knowing he wasn't the only one to be affected by Athena. Gram believed in her, and in all that spirit nonsense. He felt caught between a rock and a hard place. If he ordered Athena to go, Gram would suffer. And if he kept his word and allowed her to stay...

He stopped hammering and again wiped an arm across his brow. The therapy wasn't working today. He was building up a sweat, but he couldn't exorcise her from his thoughts. It had been four days and still he remembered her softness, the taste and feel of her mouth, the warm pressure of her body against his.

Christopher pounded the next nail with unnecessary force. He didn't like having a woman on his mind, especially a woman like Athena. She was a schemer; she had deliberately maneuvered herself into his life, she was ready to achieve her goal by using any available tool—even her body.

Roughly he pulled the last board into place. He should have told her to go. He had merely compounded his original mistake by allowing her more time at Burke House. He'd attempted to avoid her, he'd tried being coolly civil. Neither approach worked. No matter what he did she remained on his mind, always present just beneath the level of his consciousness, ready to pop up when he least expected. He didn't like it. He didn't like the feeling of being out of control.

Damn the woman! Christopher picked up his tools and walked to the nearest faucet. Taking off his hard hat, he ducked his head and let cold water pour over his hair and face. If only he could wash Athena out of his mind this easily, he thought wryly. If he'd thought to end the MacKay business by allowing her to come to Scotland, his strategy had badly backfired. He hadn't put an end to anything. Instead he'd started something infinitely more disturbing. Something, he admitted, muttering a curse, he wasn't at all sure he knew how to handle.

As a special treat, Athena suggested that she and Gram have lunch in the garden. The weather was too beautiful to waste time inside the house. Less than a week ago they'd been snowed in. Today the countryside seemed alive with spring; there were buds on the trees, and they were surrounded by the lively chatter of birds.

"It's beautiful, isn't it?" Athena closed her eyes. Behind them she could hear the gentle pounding of the surf against the cliff. The sun felt warm on her face, the air

brisk and tinged with salt. She breathed deeply and relaxed.

"You look tired, lass." Athena looked up to find Gram
studying her over rimless glasses. "You've been spendin'
so much time outside my door at night I don't think you're
gettin' enough sleep."

"Your friend keeps late hours," Athena told her affa-
bly.

"Aye. Still, you've got me worried. Much as I want to
be rid of that old devil, I won't have it at your expense."

"I'm fine, Gram, really. And we're making progress."

Gram leaned forward eagerly. "Do you think so?"

"Absolutely. We know you're not imagining the footsteps or the increased cold in the air. My instruments bear
that out. And we have the pictures, don't forget." She
stretched out in her chair and slipped off her shoes. It felt
good to wriggle her toes in the grass. "Now all we have to
do is discover what's making the disturbance and why."

"Och! There's no mystery there. It's Angus MacKay—
no doubt about it. And I can't say I care much why he's
doin' it, only that he stops."

"But that's just it," Athena said patiently. "Unless we
find out why he feels compelled to reenact the last hours
of his life, we won't know how to dispatch him."

"What do you mean, dispatch him?" Gran cocked her
small head at Athena. "Where would you be sendin'
him?"

"To his rest, hopefully." She smiled at the old lady.
"Something must have happened to prevent him from
going on—after his death. For some reason his spirit remains tied to Burke House. We have to find out why and
then try to release him."

"Can't you just tell him he's missed the boat by about
three hundred years and be done with it?"

Athena laughed. "I wish it were as simple as that." She reached across the table and patted Gram's hand. "Don't worry. We'll do it. It's just going to take a little more time."

But how much more?"

That was the question on Athena's mind that night as she ate a solitary dinner in the dining room. Christopher had called to say he would be home late. Gram had pleaded a headache and retired early. Left to her own devices, Athena found she could only pick at the lovely meal. The house was too empty tonight. Too quiet.

Without Christopher.

Athena sighed, and went to drink her coffee in the library. Again her thoughts had gone to him, just as they had all week. The long hours each night outside Gram's room had only given her more time to think, quiet time when she was forced to examine her feelings honestly and without excuses. She did care about him. Megan had extracted the truth, but only now was Athena able to accept it. Her preoccupation with Christopher was chronic—and probably incurable.

It began prior to her talk with Megan Begley. It had probably started before her stormy confrontation with him that night in his study. Athena reached for the poker and stirred the fire. Most likely she'd fallen in love with Christopher that afternoon in Kildrurry. She remembered her initial glimpse of him. How he'd taken her breath away—the medieval Viking, the sun streaking through his hair like tongues of fire. If there was any such thing as love at first sight, she'd been lost long before the battle ever began.

She threw herself into a chair. No, the feeling wasn't going to go away. And it wasn't going to get any better. She understood now the events that had etched the lines of bitterness in his face, and her heart went out to the little boy and the man he had become. But understanding couldn't breach the gap between them. It could only make the futility of the situation brutally clear. Christopher had spent a lifetime learning to hide his emotions. He would never let her in.

So it was an impasse. Their fates were sealed in a past that might never be untangled. Christopher couldn't trust. She couldn't forget.

The old grandfather's clock struck ten. Athena yawned and stretched and thought of the hours still ahead of her. Gram was right, she was tired. The long days and even longer nights were taking their toll. Yet she couldn't stop. Already a week had passed. She couldn't afford to let up until she had found what she was looking for.

Which was what? she asked herself, staring into the fire. What *was* she looking for? The mystery was 350 years old, she reminded herself realistically. How in the world could she hope to solve it now? She might rid Gram of her "ghost"—there was a reasonable hope of doing that. But how could she prove the MacKays' claim to Kildrurry? Seven days gone and she still hadn't a clue.

All right, she told herself, while going upstairs. First things first. Take care of Gram, then worry about Kildrurry. To do that, Athena had already decided that a move was in order. The bedroom across the hall from Gram's was unused. It made far more sense for her to sleep there, on the spot, rather than upstairs and down a long maze of corridors. That afternoon she'd moved her equipment into the room, now she brought down some of her clothes and toilet articles. If she had to be up half the night, she decided she could at least be more comfortable.

Changing into her nightgown and robe, Athena drew a chair up to the door of the spare bedroom. She checked to make certain Gram was asleep, turned out the hall lights and prepared to wait.

By the time he placed the key in the door, Christopher had put in a sixteen-hour day, seven of them at a construction site, the last four dining with a group of businessmen who were backing the new cultural center in Kirkcaldy.

He went directly to the stairs. After he checked Gram, he would drop into bed. He knew his long day was a form of escape, but he made no apologies. In two weeks Athena would be gone. Until then, the only way he knew to cope with having her beneath his roof was to put as much distance between them as possible.

He found her asleep in the chair, her feet and legs uncovered where the robe had come apart. Her head rested awkwardly against the back of the chair. Some curls had fallen across her face, partially covering one eye. Her camera dangled from her extended right arm, the strap wound loosely about her wrist.

For a long moment he stood looking down at her. She appeared so innocent that he was taken aback. She was like a little girl who'd fallen asleep waiting to catch a glimpse of Santa Claus. Once more she had taken him unawares. There was nothing of the seductress about her now. Only quiet beauty and, yes, he thought with wonder, vulnerability.

Bending over, he brushed the curls from her face and gently lifted her into his arms. She muttered something, then pulled closer to him, nestling in the crook of his shoulder. There was something so trusting, so childlike about the gesture that Christopher was touched with a warmth that surprised him. He didn't want to put her down. She felt right in his arms, as if she belonged there.

She stirred again, and in her sleep turned her head into his chest and wrapped her arms around his shoulders. He felt the soft pressure of her breasts against his shirt and with it came a quick stab of desire. He was torn. One part of him wanted to take her to his room and make love to her, and once and for all be free of this obsession. Another part of him argued to put her down before it was too late.

Even as he stood undecided in the doorway, he knew he was losing the battle. The evasive scent of spring that always seemed to surround her blurred his senses, the warm, soft feel of her skin against him made him forget all the reasons he should leave. He wanted to make love to her. Already his body was growing hard with need. He wanted to arouse her slowly from her sleep and feel her stir to life beneath his fingers. He wanted to unleash the passion within her he sensed could be his.

"Christopher?"

She was looking up at him, her eyes still veiled with sleep. It was absolute madness standing here holding her this way. He had to put her down, he told himself. Put her down, close the door and get out!

Before he could change his mind, Christopher carried her over to the bed and laid her on top of the spread. But when he tried to move her arms from around his neck, she sighed and pulled him down beside her. Awkwardly he lay next to her. Her arms were still holding him, and she'd turned her head until it was resting in the crook of his shoulder. Her scent and the feel of her body against him were nearly overpowering. It was all he could do not to move, to still the hands that wanted to touch her, awaken her, make love to her, and the devil take tomorrow.

Christopher took a long, even breath, trying to ignore the hard knot of desire that was firing his loins. When she stirred and pressed even closer against him, he felt the last of his fragile control slipping.

He tried to untangle her arms from around his neck, murmuring softly, "Athena, I have to go."

Slowly her eyes opened to stare at him. "Christopher?" Her voice was thick from sleep, and she looked disoriented. "Where are we?"

"In the room across from Gram's," he whispered. "You were asleep on the chair." He felt the warm caress of her breath on his face and fought to keep from kissing her. "You looked cold so I . . . I put you to bed."

"Oh." He could see that she was still trying to clear her head. "What time is it?"

"After one." He could feel the softness of her breast against his side. In another moment it would be too late. "Athena, I have to go."

"Yes."

But neither of them moved. She was looking up at him, and he saw his own desire reflected in her eyes. She wanted him. She had grasped the inevitability of the situation even as he still lay fighting it. Then the fragile line was crossed, and Christopher knew there could be no turning back. No matter what happened tomorrow, he had to have her tonight. There was no longer a choice.

For Athena there had never been a choice. Wakening in his arms had been a sweet extension of her dream. She felt warm and safe lying cradled against his body. She belonged there. It seemed to her as if she had always belonged there.

"I want you, Athena," he murmured huskily into her hair.

"Yes. I know." Her sigh embraced his cheek. "I want you, too." She turned, seeking him, her arms tightening on his neck.

"Dear Lord... Athena!"

Then the time for words was past and they came together as each of them knew they would, knew they must. Her hands became twisted in his hair and she pulled him closer, wanting to feel, to taste, to experience everything about him. She couldn't explain the urgency that possessed her, nor did she care. Mindlessly she gave in to it, allowing it to lead to heights of bliss she had never known before.

She didn't want to think, she didn't want to consider the right or the wrong of what they were doing. Old hurts and injuries seemed suddenly not to matter. All that existed now were his lips on hers, his hard chest crushing her breasts, the ache growing inside her that demanded to be satisfied.

Christopher couldn't get enough of her lips. They were soft and silky. Gently he caught her bottom lip between his teeth and felt her body quiver as he ran his tongue over its roundness. When he could hold off no longer, he allowed his tongue free rein to ravage her mouth. He wanted to know every inch of it, every sweet, secret corner.

As his tongue hungrily plundered, Athena's hands moved from his shoulders to fumble with his tie, somehow undoing the knot and slipping it from his neck. Her fingers shook as the buttons on his shirt evaded her.

"Easy, love. Easy," he murmured, raising her off the bed until he could ease her arms out of the robe. Tossing it aside, he tugged off her nightgown, too eager to be patient, too consumed with her to wait. When she lay naked beside him he was perfectly still, gazing at her in the moonlight as if he had never seen a woman before. And truly, he had never seen one like this. She was breathtaking—her skin a smooth, milky satin, her breasts round and firm and dusky rose at the tips, her legs, long, graceful and holding, at their summit, the promise of paradise. She was like an exquisite masterpiece executed by a master painter.

For Athena there were his heady textures—the soft cotton of his shirt against her breasts, the maddening, sensuous scatch of his wool pants against her hips and legs, the feel of his hands, his fingers, touching her, firing her. Then his clothes became a distraction. She had to feel more of him. She yearned for the searing intoxication that came of flesh touching flesh.

He felt her fingers yanking on his shirt and guided them down until the buttons were managed and she had the freedom to roam the hard, ropy expanse of his chest. With every move of her fingers the ache inside him grew until he was afraid he would explode. This kind of urgency was new to him. He had lusted for many women, but never like this. Always before, part of him had remained detached from the passion; it was controlled, planned, a matter of biological need.

Tonight he was consumed, it was in his blood, his bones, the very core of his being. He was burning up. Never had he wanted to possess a woman like this. He needed to make her completely, totally his!

Athena shuddered as his hands seemed to be everywhere at once, awakening her, making her acutely aware of her own femininity. His fingers roamed the hills and valleys of her body, lingering to explore the sensitive areas that Athena had not known existed. When his lips followed the devastating path of his hands, she thought she would surely go mad. She had never felt so alive, so desired.

Leisurely his tongue circled the dark silhouette of a nipple, and it peaked and grew hard in his mouth. Without hurrying, he moved to her other breast to describe equally

torturous patterns that left her writhing beneath the onslaught.

Athena felt dizzy. There were too many sensations as-
sailing her at once. In order to regain her equilibrium, she
buried her hands in the thick, curly mat of his chest, but
it made it worse, only increased her disorientation. All ra-
tionality had gone, leaving only emotion, a raw, hungry
need to be fulfilled, to be made whole. She felt her breasts
grow full and taut beneath the steady persuasiveness of his
mouth and she gloried in it. She moaned softly and let him
take her slowly deeper and deeper into the swirling eddy.

His fingers pressed into the firm softness of her hips,
and as his lips traveled even lower, her body arched ach-
ingly into his. She writhed, she twisted, the knot in her
stomach was becoming unbearable.

"You taste so good," he breathed, burying his mouth in
the gently rounded firmness of her stomach. "Like wild-
flowers. Like spring." It was true. Her scent followed him
everywhere. He'd tried to escape it at the construction site
today, at the office, even at dinner. But always it was there,
teasing him, reaching out to him when he least expected.
She was like a heady drug. And he was addicted.

His mouth traveled lower. He felt shudders like tiny
ripples beneath his hands when he reached the soft, warm
apex of her femininity. Her reaction to him was making it
very hard to wait. His body was clamoring for her, demanding satisfaction. But he wanted her satisfaction first.
He wanted to feel her blaze to life beneath him. He wanted
it to be like nothing she had ever known before or would
ever experience again. He wanted her to always remember
the night she surrendered to him!

"Christopher. Please—" Athena gasped at what he was
doing to her, as ripple after ripple of pleasure swept
through her. She closed her eyes tightly, feeling as if she

were flying apart into a million pieces. How long could it last? How long could she bear this beautiful, aching torture? Her hands clutched his shoulders, twisted in his hair. She couldn't catch her breath. She felt as if she were going to explode.

Christopher caressed the moist dampness between her thighs and felt a thrill of purely male satisfaction. He looked up, and through the pale spill of moonlight he could see that her eyes were tightly closed, her face straining with passion. He had brought her to this, he thought in wonder. She wanted him. She was ready for him.

Then he was lying beside her, his hands reaching for her firm, full breasts. He fought the storm building inside him. He couldn't last much longer. Yet he wanted it to be perfect. He wanted her never to forget.

Christopher's breath caught as her hands again grasped his shoulders. Lightly she ran her nails across the broad expanse of his chest, then onto the lean, flat line of his abdomen. When her fingers tentatively explored even lower to find the hard, throbbing seat of his passion, he thought he would go out of his mind.

"I don't think I . . . can wait any longer." His voice was a breathless husk against her mouth. "You feel so good. Tell me . . . tell me that you want me, Athena. I have to hear you say it."

"Yes. Oh, yes." She had no breath left. She had no thought left. There was nothing but his body on hers, his heart pounding into her breasts. She'd had no idea it could be like this. She was burning up. She was on fire. "Yes, Christopher. God, yes. I want you."

He did not wait to hear more. Nudging apart her legs, he shaped his hands on the soft, giving flesh of her buttocks and pulled her upward, into him. He heard her soft cry as he thrust himself completely into her moist softness. She was his. The voice inside him kept pace with his rhythm. Finally, tonight, she was his!

The climax came almost immediately. They were both deluged, drowned in a sea of sensations. Athena couldn't breathe, she could only move against him, matching his pace, soaring to heights beyond her wildest imagination. When it was over they clung to each other, exhausted. They were drained—there was nothing left to give.

Her heart thudded against his chest. Their bodies were damp and their breath came in ragged gasps. Athena felt him shift and she opened her eyes to find him looking down on her. She saw surprise and wonderment on his face. She felt inside her heart but could find no regrets. She loved him. For tonight that was enough. Sighing softly, Athena closed her eyes again and allowed herself to drift in the sweet afterglow of contentment.

Christopher studied her in the moonlight. His body was relaxed but his mind was in turmoil. She was warm and soft beneath him, and he could feel the thud of her heart against his own. He had just had her and he wanted her again.

Very gently, he moved his weight until he was lying next to her. She sighed in her sleep and moved with him, remaining curled in his arms, her hand resting on his heart. For the second time that night he was touched so profoundly that it surprised him. How could she look so innocent, so vulnerable, when she had just caused him to lose himself in a way he had never before experienced?

Watching her, Christopher attempted to deal with his feelings. He had never been caught up like that before. He had wanted her to surrender. He had wanted her never to forget. He'd been a fool. In the end it had been *he* who had surrendered. He would be the one who would never forget.

She sighed and moved closer into the crook of his arm. Without thinking he gently stroked her skin until he felt it tremble beneath his touch. He felt his own reaction, hard and immediate.

"Damn you, Athena," he murmured, turning her into him. "I can't get enough of you. You've bewitched me."

"Bewitching handsome men is part of my job," she murmured, coming fully awake. She smiled up at him, feeling his arousal. "Would you like me to reverse the spell?"

He looked down and saw the laughter in her eyes. His heart instantly lightened, as if she'd brought her own private sunshine into the room. All the self-doubts and anger flowed out of him as he smiled down at her. "Never," he said, reaching for her lips. "Not a chance."

Seven

I shot these last night." Her face colored slightly. "About an hour before you, ah, woke me up."

They were standing in Athena's makeshift darkroom. Christopher was studying the prints in the faint red light as they came out of the hypo. "You've taken some fairly clear shots of the hallway. What's unusual about them?"

Athena pointed to a foggy area in one of the prints. "Look, in this one there's a luminescence in the center of the corridor—like a ball of light."

He looked closer at the picture, then shook his head. "Your film is clouded."

She made a frustrated sound. "If the roll is clouded then why doesn't this hazy light appear on all the pictures?"

"Perhaps only one part of the roll was affected. Or there may be something wrong with your camera."

Athena muttered beneath her breath as she sorted through the photos to pick out last night's "control" pictures, the shots she always took just prior to and immediately after a session to ensure that her camera was functioning properly. She spread the prints out in front of him. "These shots of the hallway are from the same roll, taken only minutes before and after the foggy prints. Look closely. There's no sign of distortion or unexplained light."

He shook his head. "There must be a logical explanation."

"There is! You just don't want to admit it. Something's there—in the hall." When he continued to shake his head, she went on impatiently, "I know that isn't the explanation you're looking for, but that doesn't make it less valid." She turned off the light and opened the door. "Come on. I want to show you something else."

Athena took him down the hallway to her room. Inside, she opened a file and spread out a collection of printouts.

"These figures are from the photocells I placed along the corridor outside Gram's room. Utilizing a variety of filters, I've been able to test several portions of the light spectrum." She reached for a stack of photographs. "These pictures are dated and I've noted the exact time they were taken. They correspond almost perfectly with the data from these printout sheets."

"You're trying to tell me these readings substantiate your photographs?"

"You can see for yourself that they do." Why was it so difficult for some people to accept a fact even when the evidence was staring them in the eyes? She laid out the thermistor readings. "See? As the light grew closer, the temperature dropped several degrees. Here, at the light's closest point, it dropped even lower."

"This is a drafty house, Athena. The temperature fluctuates constantly, especially in the hallways."

"What about the luminescent light?" she challenged. "You can't explain that away with a draft."

"No," he agreed calmly. "But I can cite dozens of instances where film has been defective or a camera has functioned improperly. You may even have caught some flashes of lightning or simply overexposed the film."

"Overexposed it! Twenty-two times? That's how many pictures I have showing an unexplained light, Christopher. And three times that many have been 'normally' exposed." She looked up at him defiantly. "How do you explain that?"

The humorous glint in his blue eyes merely stoked her indignation. She'd worked more than a week to collect this data, and all he could do was look amused. "Christopher. I'm serious!"

"I know you are." He pulled her into his arms, brushing some curls off her forehead. "Has anyone ever told you how lovely you are?"

"You're changing the subject." She tried not to respond to the persuasive touch of his hands on her back. "Christopher, I'm trying to make a point here."

"So am I."

Her protest was lost in the power of his kiss. She tried to fight it, but knew it was hopeless. His arms had a way of blotting out her usual common sense. "It's...it's ten o'clock in the morning," she managed when he broke off the embrace to scoop her into his arms.

"A quarter after." He carried her to the bed.

"But I have more to show you."

"And I have a few things to show you." He laid her gently on top of the quilt, then eased his powerful body down beside her. "It's my turn."

"But the printouts—"

"Later."

Then his mouth was on hers and her mind whirled with conflicting sensations. She felt herself slowly sinking into a chasm of desire. How did he do it? she wondered vaguely, then even that thought slipped away. Suddenly her world revolved around his lips, his hands, the feel of his hard chest against her cheek.

He had to fight the urge to crush her against him. Last night he thought he'd had his fill of her. Today he knew that was wrong. He still needed her, perhaps more desperately than before. But the need was subtly different. This morning he wanted time to really know her. Suddenly that was very important to him.

"Just relax," he breathed. "We have all the time in the world."

Cupping her face in his hands, he paused and looked into her eyes. "Today I want to see you," he murmured. "I want to watch your eyes, I want to see your skin flush while I make love to you. I want to know what you like and where, and then I want to watch you respond."

His words warmed her body and clouded her brain. Why did he have this power over her? His hand touched her cheek and she trembled. One touch, she thought in wonder. Just one touch and her whole body cried out for him.

His hands slipped beneath her sweater, wanting to feel her skin. Her fingers were busy with his shirt, and when he felt their magic touch on his chest he was overcome by a wild leap of desire. Somehow he pulled off the sweater, need pushing at him as he feasted on the sweet roundness of her breasts. Unhooking her bra, he threw it to the floor. When he took her back into his arms, she seemed to melt into him.

Christopher fought to go slowly. Last night he had been driven. Again and again he had taken her, but he'd been too frenzied to savor her, to explore her fully, leisurely. The need was still driving him, but this time he would not be hurried. He would control the fever. He would discover all there was to know about her.

"I . . . I think you're doing it very well." His hand ran down her shoulders, hesitating briefly to feather over her breasts, then down to her waist. She trembled. "Making . . . making your point, I mean."

"Good." His lips were following the path of his hands and his voice was muffled. He said something else, but the words were lost to other, more extraordinary, sensations.

Then her body was throbbing for him and it was no longer important. She discovered there were times when words didn't matter at all.

Athena stood in the library and decided she had to go to Edinburgh. *Campbell's Chronicle of Scottish Clans* was open in front of her. Over the past week she had read and reread the MacKay entry until she knew it by heart. The time had come, she decided, to establish whether or not it was true.

Casually she mentioned her plans at dinner. To her surprise, and secret dismay, Christopher suggested going with her.

"I blame myself for not taking you there sooner. You haven't seen much of Scotland stuck out here on the edge of nowwhere."

"That's all right. I didn't come to here to sightsee." She smiled at him nervously, not knowing how to tell him she'd rather go alone. How could she dig for evidence to disprove the Burke story with Christopher looking over her shoulder. "Actually, I thought I'd spend some time at the library."

"I see. And you think I might be in the way."

"Of course not." She stopped and looked at him sheepishly. "Well, not in the way, exactly. More of a...a distraction. Anyway, I don't want to take you away from your work."

"Tomorrow's Saturday," he reminded her. "I have nothing so pressing it can't wait until Monday. And there's a party I should attend. We could make a weekend of it."

"A party?" Athena looked at him in surprise. She had difficulty picturing Christopher in that sort of social setting. He seemed too serious, too much the loner.

He smiled as if reading her thoughts. "At first I'd planned to skip the party. Now I think it might be interesting after all. You can run interference for me."

"You mean save you from boring men, licentious women and overbearing matrons playing Cupid."

He reached over and covered her hand with his own. "That's the general idea."

Athena felt his warmth flowing into her cold fingers. She wanted to be with him, away from Burke House, away from the ghosts of the past. She wanted to be totally alone with him for the first—perhaps the *only* time.

She smiled, burying practical considerations, knowing that once again she was putting off reality until tomorrow. What would happen, she wondered, when tomorrow finally arrived?

"I've never had the job of bodyguard," she told him. "It sounds like it might be fun."

He went with her to the Edinburgh library. By tacit agreement, neither of them spoke of the purpose of her visit, although Athena realized from the way he unerringly led her to the proper floor of the building that Christopher knew. The librarian in charge directed them to a row of stacks.

"I'm afraid you may find it difficult to find what you're looking for," she told Athena regretfully. "General information covering seventeenth-century border-clan history is extensive. However, specific details pertaining to a particular clan may be harder to find."

Several hours later, Athena reluctantly agreed. Together they had pored over dozens of histories, some of them enormous, tedious volumes. To Christopher's credit, he worked diligently, without comment or complaint. If he was tempted to take an "I told you so" attitude toward the project, he thankfully kept the thoughts to himself.

Late in the afternoon, Athena finally admitted defeat. "I've read about the Burke-MacKay feud until I'm blue in the face. And I haven't found a single word about what happened that Christmas Eve." She was sitting back in her chair, books scattered on the table in front of her. Her hands were dirty and there was a dark smudge on her cheek. Chestnut curls flew in disarray about her face from running her fingers through her hair in frustration. Christopher thought she looked lovely.

"No one can say you haven't tried," he said. "And the librarian did warn that it might be difficult to find."

"Yes, but you'd think there'd be *something* in all this." She swept her hand at the books. "Just one or two sentences. That's all I ask."

"We could come back next week."

She smiled wearily over the mountain of books. "Either you're unbelievably patient or you're a glutton for punishment." She studied him frankly. "Why are you doing this, Christopher? You don't expect me to find anything."

"Because I want you to be satisfied. I don't want you left with any lingering doubts about what happened."

"But I do have doubts." Again she ran her finger
through her hair, causing the curls to scatter in even mor
disorder. She blew several locks out of her eyes. "Yo
would have to have known my father. He was a remark
able man—admittedly an idealist, but scrupulously hor
est. He wouldn't have—he *couldn't* have—based th
dream of a lifetime on wishful thinking."

"Perhaps it was just that, Athena. A dream," h
pointed out gently. "People do sometimes get carried awa
with their dreams."

"Not Dad. I can't believe that."

"Can't or won't, Athena?"

He was watching her from across the table. Not for th
first time, she had the uncomfortable feeling that he coul
guess what she was thinking. She shook her head and sud
denly felt very tired. "I don't know, Christopher. I don
want it to be true. But—I just don't know."

He stood, scraping back his chair. "Come on. It's bee
a long day. It's time to go."

Christopher's apartment was small but had a feeling o
intimacy that was lacking at Burke House. It stood o
High Street and commanded a breathtaking view of Edi
burgh Castle, which was formidably perched high abov
the city atop an extinct volcano. Athena stood at the wir
dow, awed by the fifteen hundred years of history sprea
out below her. "It's wonderful," she murmured.

"Yes, it is, isn't it?" He had come to stand quietly b
hind her, his hands resting lightly on her shoulders. Sl
had combed her mass of curls, but they still flew ever
which way about her head in the way he loved. He felt h
warmth and breathed deeply of the fresh flower scent th
seemed always to surround her. He had forgotten how e
citing Edinburgh could be. Discovering it through her ey
made it seem as if he was seeing it again for the first tim

She turned her head. "You're not looking at the city at all."

"I'd much rather look at you." His hands slipped around her waist to pull her into his arms. Here, away from the castle, he thought she would be his, without complications, without ancient feuds lurking in the shadows. But nothing was changed. The doubts were still there. Even here he felt the impossible need to hold her to him, to keep her from the rest of the world.

"You're spoiled," she accused. "You're used to all this and you'll soon tire of looking at me, as well."

He turned her around until she was facing him, then searched her eyes. "Will I, Athena? I've wondered about that."

His seriousness made her uncomfortable. They only had this weekend. For these two days only she wanted to pretend they were like any other lovers. She wanted the intimacy, the enjoyment, the sharing of each other, unencumbered by doubts or fears of the future. She moved into his arms and closed her eyes. "Don't wonder about anything, Christopher. Not now. Let's leave the questions for later."

And because he wanted to pretend with her, he held back his uncertainties. She was right. Later was time enough for questions.

He caressed her hair and felt the accelerated beat of her heart against his chest. Placing a finger beneath her chin, he drew up her face. "Have I told you yet today that you're very beautiful?"

"Not for two minutes at least." Without looking away from his eyes, she helped him out of his jacket.

"I must be slipping." His hands were on the zipper of her dress. With one smooth movement, he pulled it down below her waist.

She unknotted his tie and let it drop onto the carpet. His lips momentarily caused her to pause at the top button to his shirt. "Yes, you must. What am I going to do with you?" she whispered a minute later, continuing with the task.

"I'm sure you'll think of something," he murmured. He nibbled at her ear, then let his lips roam hungrily to the deep, warm valley between her breasts. In another moment her slip and bra lay beside his jacket and tie.

She glanced behind them at the window. "Anyone looking up here from the street could see us."

"Their treat," he growled softly. After his shirt had joined the growing pile of clothes on the floor, he ran his hands lingeringly down the curves of her breasts, then farther to the slender indentation of her waist and the firm fullness of her hips. His soft groan acted as a heady aphrodisiac to Athena's already soaring need.

Trembling now, she fumbled with the clasp of his belt. When he stood clad only in his snug-fitting briefs, she sighed at the blatant evidence of his arousal. "You're not bad yourself," she told him. She had a sudden need to feel him, to know his need more intimately. Rising on tiptoe, she put her arms around his neck and pressed her body tightly against him. His strength reassured her, it stimulated her, it made her complete. She wished tomorrow would never come. "I want to be with you like this forever," she whispered desperately.

Forever. Christopher wondered fleetingly if there was any such thing, then stopped thinking of anything but the moment. He cupped the fragile weight of a breast, marveling at its firm, perfect shape and fullness. Everything about her was just as it should be. "You're exquisite," he murmured.

Athena had never thought of herself as either beautiful or exquisite, but suddenly that was exactly how she felt. Moaning, she strained against him, letting her breasts fill his large, powerful hands. Christopher felt her nipples grow into hard, erect buds, and he experienced a sharp stab of desire. Impatient now, he reached for the wisp of her panties and slid them down the long, smooth length of her legs.

His mouth came back to hers, hungry and urgent. She arched into him, dizzy from a kiss that seemed to rock her all the way to the core of her being. Her needs made it impossible to think. Pure instinct drove her hands to tug off his briefs until no barriers remained between them. Again and again their lips met, the tasting breathless and desperate.

Control was slipping from him. Athena's fingers were on his back, and he felt the light scratch of her nails between his shoulder blades. Sweeping her into his arms, he carried her to the bed. For a moment he held her motionless in his embrace before lowering her to the spread. She nibbled at the corded muscles straining in his neck, and he thrilled to the taut fullness of the breasts that pressed against his chest. Her skin was cool satin in his work-roughened hands, her breath a warm, sweet caress in his hair. He felt her heart pounding in unison with his own.

Unable to wait any longer, he dropped beside her, too driven now to be gentle. He watched her face as he entered her. The fading light of day turned her skin a deep, dusky gold. Her eyes were closed as she arched up to meet him, her lips parted, her breaths ragged and shallow. He kept his strokes slow and deep, wanting the moment to last, loving the waves of passion that rippled her body, reveling in her soft moans of pleasure.

Then his pace quickened as he was engulfed by her. He was drowning in her softness and was powerless to save himself. All that mattered was the feel of her and his need to be whole again.

With a last lingering cry, they soared and crested. Nothing existed beyond the whirlwind into which they'd been swept. Each was lost in the excruciating joy of the other. For a beautiful, brief period of time, that was enough.

"Everyone's talking about Christopher's 'ghost hunter.'" The short, plump matron who had introduced herself as Mildred St. Giles was clutching Athena's arm in a way that made her very uncomfortable. "I just couldn't wait to meet you."

"I'm flattered, Mrs. St. Giles." Athena smiled and tried unsuccessfully to extricate her arm. Despite her small stature, the woman had a grip of steel.

"You must tell me about your work, dear. How *do* you go about catching ghosts? It sounds absolutely fascinating!"

"Actually, I don't catch them, Mrs. St. Giles." Athena looked somewhat desperately around the room for some sign of Christopher. She'd seen nothing of him since William Begley cornered him earlier and whisked him off to talk business. "I investigate paranormal activity."

"You mean like poltergeists and flying saucers?"

"Sometimes poltergeists," Athena answered. "UFO's are a bit out of my line."

The woman looked disappointed. "Really? A friend of mine had a very peculiar experience a few years ago." Before Athena could think of a polite excuse to move away, Mrs. St. Giles had launched into her story. It was a relief to hear a familiar voice call out her name a few minutes later.

"There you are, Athena. I've been looking all over for you."

Athena smiled her thanks at Megan Begley and started to introduce her to Mrs. St. Giles.

"We've been friends for years," Megan told her. She took the older woman's hand. "You won't mind if I steal Athena away for a moment, will you, Mildred? There's someone I want her to meet."

"I owe you a very big favor," Athena said, gratefully accepting a champagne cocktail from a passing waiter. Megan had led her into another, equally crowded room. This time, Athena surveyed the guests with the comfortable assurance that Megan was at hand to stave off the more aggressive of their number.

"You were beginning to look desperate," Megan told her, capturing a passing canapé. "By the way, where's Christopher? He hasn't deserted you?"

"Your brother commandeered him. He said something about unexpected business and promised to return him in ten minutes."

"With William that could mean anything up to an hour or even more." She stopped a waiter and heaped caviar onto a thin cracker and savored it appreciatively. "That's it," she vowed, wiping her scarlet-tipped fingers on a napkin. "I've already used up two full days' worth of calories." She took Athena's arm. "Come on, love. There really is someone I want you to meet."

Megan led her across the room to an attractive young man in his early thirties. Just under six feet, he had a round face and bright, cheerful gray eyes. A short brown beard and mustache concealed a triangular-shaped jaw and a

full, generous mouth. Athena thought he looked vaguely
familiar and she wondered if they had met before.

"Dr. Peter Scott, I'd like you to meet Athena MacKay.
Athena, Peter Scott, one of your colleagues. Peter holds
his doctorate in psychology, but a year or so ago he was
associated with the parapsychology unit at the University
of Edinburgh."

"Dr. Scott, I'm honored to meet you." Athena took the
man's hand with honest pleasure. "No wonder your name
seemed familiar. I've seen it frequently in the parapsychology journals."

"Peter is in Edinburgh on holiday," Megan told her.
"He's been conducting some sort of psychic studies in
London."

"We're doing experiments in psychokinesis." He
laughed at Megan's raised eyebrow. "It sounds worse than
it is. We study the direct influence of mind on matter
without an intermediate physical energy or instrumenta-
tion."

Megan shook her head. "Sorry, Peter, but that's even
worse than it sounds. Will you two excuse me? I see a
friend I can talk with on the thornier problems of next
year's skirt length." She flashed her dazzling smile. "I'll
leave you to your psycho—whatever."

"Quite a lady," Scott commented as Megan floated
away from them.

"She is, isn't she?" On closer inspection she thought
Peter Scott was older than she'd first guessed, perhaps in
his mid to late thirties. There was a boyish look about him
that made him appear younger.

"I read your article in *World Psychology*," he told her.
"It was very impressive."

Athena looked surprised. "That was published two years ago, Dr. Scott. It was a preliminary study for my doctoral thesis. I'm surprised you remember."

"Peter, please. And I'll call you Athena, if I may. I liked the way you related the dream and reverie states to psychic or paranormal phenomena. Peripherally, I'm concerned with that in my own experiments." He grinned. "I envy you. You have a wonderful way with words. Putting my thoughts on paper is pure, unadulterated torture."

She returned his smile. "I know the feeling, believe me. It took me weeks to write that article."

"Megan tells me you're in Edinburgh for professional reasons."

"I'm staying in North Berwick, actually. At Burke House." She reached for a fresh glass of champagne.

He raised one dark eyebrow. "Ah, Burke House. Then it must be the infamous Angus MacKay who's brought you here."

Athena paused, her glass halfway to her lips. "You know about him then."

He lowered his voice dramatically. "I know that old Angus's spirit is reputed to stalk Burke House seeking retribution." He laughed. "Scotland is full of restless spirits looking for revenge. All part of its charm."

"Can you tell me the legend, Peter?"

"Surely you've heard the story already."

"Since I was a little girl. But I'd really like to hear it again. From you."

"There's more than one version, you know. I doubt that anyone knows what really happened."

"To which theory do you subscribe?" she asked, watching him closely.

"To be honest with you, I haven't given it much thought. I suppose the most widely accepted version is that Angus was enticed into one too many dice games."

Athena felt her heart sink. "Then you think he lost everything gambling."

He heard the disappointment in her voice. "Who knows? It's been what, three, four hundred years?"

"Three hundred and fifty. I've been unable to find evidence to support *any* of the theories. Why do you suppose the gambling one is so popular?"

"Who knows? Some seventeenth-century preacher probably happened upon it and decided it made a good case against the evils of gambling. It certainly has its share of melodrama, doesn't it?" He pulled a thin gold case out of his pocket, extracted a cigarette and lit it with a matching gold lighter. Taking a long drag, he exhaled and said, "You know, Athena, most of these old clan stories come down to us by word of mouth. Some have been made into ballads, others simply filter down through families. I have no idea if one version of the MacKay story is more valid than another. Is it that important to you?"

"Yes," she told him quietly. "I'm afraid it is."

"Ah, yes," he said with sudden insight. "Kildrurry was the Clan MacKay seat, wasn't it? I read that it's to be torn down for a golf course, although it seems to me that Scotland already has more than its share of those already."

"They're breaking ground in one week."

"And you're out to save Kildrurry from this infamous fate."

She smiled at him, but couldn't mask the frustration in her eyes. "I'm trying. So far I haven't been very successful."

"I suppose you've tried the library."

"All afternoon. No luck."

"And the office of public records?" he suggested. "You might do better there."

"I thought that would be my next line of attack." She sipped her champagne. "Do you suppose their records date back that far?"

"One thing you'll find out about the Scots," he said with a smile, "they rarely throw anything away that can be saved. If they've ever had the deed, and it hasn't been destroyed in a fire or similar act of nature, you can rest assured it's still there."

"Then that's my next move." She smiled with more confidence than she was feeling.

"And if you fail to find something there, as well?"

She shrugged sadly. "Then I guess Scotland will have one more golf course."

Christopher weaved his way through the crowd, deftly dodging several people who would have wanted him to talk. He stopped when he spied her standing with a bearded man by the fireplace. Athena was holding a glass of champagne and laughing. The man's hand was resting lightly on her arm. Athena looked up and saw him.

"I wondered if you were ever going to resurface," she said, smiling as he joined them. She turned to her companion. "Dr. Peter Scott, Sir Christopher Burke."

Christopher nodded stiffly, then watched the man remove his hand from Athena's arm and extend it to him.

"Dr. Scott," he acknowledged coolly, briefly returning the shake.

"Peter is in Edinburgh on vacation," Athena told him noticing that Christopher's manner was strained. Did they know each other? she wondered. Peter hadn't mentioned it.

"Just looking up some old friends at the university," Peter told him. He smiled at Athena. "You're fortunate to have the expertise of such a brilliant young scientist, Sir Christopher. Athena is making quite a name for herself in the field."

"Is she now?" Christopher stopped a passing waiter and took a drink. He sipped it thoughtfully.

"Peter's conducting research in London," Athena said, watching Christopher. What was the matter with him? He seemed so stiff and angry. For the second time that night, she was relieved to catch sight of Megan making her way toward them. This time she had her brother, William, in tow.

He approached Athena with a twinkling smile. "I've been given the very pleasant task of apologizing to you for monopolizing so much of Christopher's time." With an exaggerated flourish he took her hand. "And so I do. Most abjectly." He kissed her hand lightly, then turned to the two men. "There, my conscience is once again as innocent as a baby's. Hello, Peter. How are things in London?"

"As usual. Drizzly and humming with tourists."

William laughed. "The same could be said for Edinburgh. I see you've met Athena."

"We've spent a thoroughly enjoyable half hour exchanging ghost stories. I've just been congratulating Sir Christopher on having such a beautiful and talented investigator on the job."

"Ever since I met her I've been trying to find a ghoulie or two of my own around our house," William said.

While everyone laughed, Athena felt Christopher's hand on her elbow. "It's been a long day," he told the others. "You won't mind if Athena and I slip out while no one's looking."

"What was that all about?" she asked as they walked the half-dozen blocks to his apartment.

"I can only take crowds in short doses." They were walking slowly, her hand tucked into the crook of his arm. He wasn't happy with himself. He didn't want to care that other men found Athena attractive. Yet one more moment with that insufferable fool Peter Scott . . .

"Are you hungry?"

"Mmm," she teased. "That depends on what you have in mind."

"I meant nourishment for the body, you wanton woman." The walk was easing his tension and he looked down at her and smiled. "But I think I like your definition better."

She held his arm more tightly, and he felt the familiar gnawing ache in his loins. When am I going to get enough of her? he wondered. Pushing aside the thought, he opened the door to his apartment and took her into his arms. "Have I told you yet how ravishing you look tonight?"

"Yes, but don't let that stop you from telling me again."

Taking her coat, he led her to the bedroom. "What about dinner?" she teased.

"Dinner can wait," he murmured, slipping off her dress. His desire for her knew no boundaries. Just when he thought he had it under control it was back, more rapacious than before. "Right now I have another appetite that is far more ravenous." He turned off the light and took her into his arms.

Eight

Athena awakened to the sound of closing drawers. Slowly she opened her eyes and focused on Christopher, naked from the waist up, standing in front of the dresser pulling out a shirt. He grinned at her and moved over to the bed to give her a light kiss.

"Morning, sleepyhead."

She eyed the powerful play of muscles that molded his shoulders and rippled across his chest. "You have a great body," she told him sleepily, then yawned and flopped her head back onto the pillow. "But I already told you that last night. You'll get a swelled head."

"Never mind the size of my head." He ruffled her hair. "Are you going to stay in bed all day?"

She looked suspiciously toward the window. "What time is it?"

"Seven-thirty."

"In the morning?" She stared up at him. "You remember, of course, that we didn't get to sleep until after three."

He ran his finger across her forehead, loving the way her curls spilled out about her head like a disheveled halo. Her skin was still flushed from their night of lovemaking, her mouth swollen from his kisses. "Did we?" he teased. "I'd forgotten."

"Cad!" Athena raised up and tried to throw her pillow at him. He captured both her wrists in one hand and replaced the pillow with the other. "Do you like eggs or hotcakes with your bacon?"

She looked at him, confused. "What?"

"For breakfast. Eggs or hotcakes? You're going to need a good meal to get you through the day I have planned."

"Oh? And just what do you have planned?"

"A complete tour of Edinburgh, starting with the castle and moving up the Royal Mile to Holyroodhouse. From there, who knows?" Releasing her hands, he bent his head and kissed each eye. "Get up, woman," he prodded, tickling her where she was most vulnerable.

"Christopher—stop." She was laughing so hard she could hardly talk. "Stop it. I can't move."

When he finally let up, she pulled up the sheets, seeking refuge beneath the covers.

"Oh no you don't," he threatened, reaching under the sheet to resume his tickling. "Get up or I won't be responsible for the consequences."

"Hmm," came a muffled voice. "That sounds interesting."

"Uh-uh. Today I have promised to show you the capital of Scotland." He stood and jerked off the covers. "I will not be led astray."

"Spoilsport." She pulled a face at him, then stretched. "In that case get back to the kitchen. I'll take the eggs *and* the hotcakes. I never did get dinner last night. I'm starved!''

The day passed too quickly for Athena. As they explored Edinburgh, it wasn't the sights that fascinated her, it was Christopher. He was a different person—he laughed, he was relaxed, he was utterly charming. My God, she thought. In six days I'll have to leave and I'm falling more in love with him by the minute!

That evening as they drove back to Burke House, Athena watched the last glow of sun fade from the horizon. They were both quiet, each lost in their own thoughts. What's on his mind? she wondered, glancing at his hard, square profile. She felt a vague sense of depression. With every mile he seemed to lose some of the spontaneity and wonderful impulsiveness that had made the weekend so special.

She leaned her head back and sighed. She'd been wrong about Christopher. At first she'd thought he was cold and calculating, a man incapable of warmth and affection. Now she realized there was far more to him than she imagined. He could be thoughtful, caring and surprisingly vulnerable. Athena realized she didn't want to say goodbye to him.

Christopher turned his head and caught her staring. Smiling, he reached out and took her hand. ''It'll be all right, Athena,'' he told her quietly, sensing her disquiet. ''Trust me.''

Trust. Silently Athena repeated the word as they drew closer to Burke House. She wanted to trust him. She wanted to believe it would be all right.

But something inside her cried caution. Too much was unsettled, too much of the past was still unresolved. It was too early to trust, she realized. Just as it was too late to reclaim her heart.

The phone rang just as Athena was going out the door. She waited for a moment to see if Lachlan or Fiona would get it, then walked back and answered it herself.

"Hello, Athena? William Begley here. Has Christopher left for the office yet?"

"Hi, William." Athena put her purse and car keys on the Edwardian chair by the phone. "He flew to Brussels early this morning. I thought you knew."

She heard his soft curse. "He wasn't supposed to go until Wednesday."

"He received a call when we got back from Edinburgh last night that changed his plans. I believe he left a message for you."

"I'm in Petershead." He sounded annoyed. "I haven't checked with the office yet. I thought I'd try to catch Christopher first."

There was a silence at the other end of the line. "Is there something I can do to help, William?"

"Did he leave a number where he could be reached?"

"He wasn't sure where he'd be staying. He promised to call later this evening. I can let you know then."

"That'll be too late. Damn." She heard a long sigh, then, when William continued, his voice held more of its customary exuberance. "Guess I'll have to field this one myself, won't I? Thanks, Athena. I'll talk to him when he gets back."

Athena forgot all about William's call as she drove into Edinburgh. Ever since talking to Peter Scott Saturday night, she'd been itching to visit Edinburgh's office of public records. As much as she missed Christopher, she had to admit this was the perfect time to try and solve the riddle of Angus MacKay.

"If we have it, it would be on microfilm," the elderly clerk informed her. "In that room over there. It may take you awhile, though."

As Athena settled in the chair before the projector, she thought that time was the one thing she didn't have. Christopher was scheduled to return the day after tomorrow. Two days after that, her three weeks would be up. Not much time, she thought, turning on the machine. Not much time to save a heritage.

It wasn't until the following morning that she found it. She'd worked most of the morning and afternoon the day before, then checked into a hotel and spent a fretful night worrying that she might not find anything at all.

Now she sat riveted to her chair staring at the screen. There it was. After weeks of searching, there it was in front of her. The Burkes' deed to Kildrurry. Dated *February 4, 1635!*

Athena requested a photocopy of the document, then left the records office in a daze. She walked aimlessly, trying to sort things out before returning to the castle. February 4—the date echoed in her mind. *Six weeks after Christmas.* Six weeks after Angus MacKay supposedly lost Kildrurry in a dice game. It was just as her father said it would be, she thought. According to his story, Angus MacKay was captured that Christmas Eve and forced to sign over the deed to his enemies. There'd been no friendly game of chance, only cold-blooded, premeditated treachery!

Walking back to the car, Athena took a different route out of the city. She had a sudden desire to see Kildrurry, to look again at the place where it all began.

"I'm so close, Dad," she murmured. "I'm so damn close! If I can just find the last few missing pieces to the puzzle!" She needed more than just a copy of the deed. By itself, the paper did not constitute hard evidence. She needed more. She had to be able to prove what happened that night.

She was still trying to plan her next move when she reached Kildrurry. It took several minutes for her mind to comprehend what her eyes were picking up visually. A bulldozer was moving earth away from the south side of the keep. Two surveyors were working just off the road to her right, and half a dozen trucks and cars were parked in front of the drawbridge. "Oh no," she murmured in shock. "They've started on the golf course!"

Athena sat in her car and watched them, wanting to be wrong. There had to be another explanation. Yet the longer she watched, the clearer it became there was no mistake. The earth mover continued its monotonous journey over the uneven hillside. The surveyors made their calculations and the trucks, cars and workers didn't leave. The truth was inescapable. He had betrayed her. Even as he made love to her, Christopher must have been planning this last, brutal strategy. Success at any price, she thought, trying to push back the pain. Wasn't that the Burke motto? And she had been foolish enough to fall for him!

Athena drove back to the castle in a fury. Taking a turn too fast, she eased her foot off the accelerator, but continued to clutch the wheel. How could she have thought she loved him? How could she have forgotten 350 years of injustice? "The Burkes don't play fair, Athena," she muttered angrily. "Dad warned you. You should have remembered!"

When Peter Scott called her later that afternoon, professing to have something of interest to show her, Athena was glad of the opportunity to get out of the house. The psychologist took her to a small restaurant in Dirleton,

where they sat at a corner table. He listened patiently while
she vented her anger, her frustration and, finally, her hurt.
When she could no longer hold back the tears, he held her
hand and waited while she cried it out.

"Sorry," she said when she had herself under control.
"I hate to make a fool of myself."

"Are you feeling better now?"

"Actually, I am." She smiled. "You're a good psychologist. You know how to listen."

"And you're only human, Athena. Don't expect so
much of yourself."

This time she grinned. "Yes, doctor." She finished
wiping her eyes just as the waitress came with their wine.
He poured some into her glass and she took a grateful sip.
"Now that I've given you an opportunity to practice your
bedside manner, what is it you wanted to tell me? You said
it had something to do with Kildrurry."

"I think I may have come across one of the missing
pieces to your puzzle." He reached into his pocket and
pulled out a paper. Athena could see it was a photocopy of
a page from a book. "I told you that the chap I'm staying
with is a professor at the university. He also happens to be
a history buff of sorts, particularly Scottish history. When
I told him about the old clan register you found at the castle, he knew it immediately.

Athena leaned forward. "He's familiar with *Campbell's Chronicle of Scottish Clans*?"

"He's familiar with Campbell. It seems Andrew
Campbell owned the largest and most prestigious publishing house in Edinburgh during the early to mid-1800s.
Their specialty was fine old histories and biographies, that
sort of thing. His house also did a number of textbooks for
the British university system, which is the main reason my

friend remembered him." He paused and lit a cigarette. Athena suspected it was for dramatic effect. It worked.

"And?" she prodded.

"And guess who was the number-two stockholder of Campbell's company for over thirty years?" Again he paused, and when Athena looked at him blankly, he went on, "Sir Henry Simpson Burke."

"Henry Burke!" Memory clicked into place as she recalled Gram speaking of her husband's grandfather, the wealthy Burke of the mid-1800s.

"None other. It appears that Sir Henry had his very lucrative finger in any number of pies. During his lifetime, the Burkes reached the pinnacle of their power and wealth. They owned half the countryside—and from what I gathered, half its people, as well." He tapped the paper. "This is a copy of an 1845 list of Campbell Publishing Limited stockholders. Burke's name is right up there at the top."

"And you think Sir Henry put Campbell up to publishing his version of the MacKay takeover?"

"It's certainly a possibility. At the very least, Campbell was biased. At the most, he might actually have been paid to print the story. I can't imagine Burke allowing his partner to print any other version of the tale, can you?"

She shook her head slowly. The pieces were coming together. If she didn't like the picture they were forming, she would have to deal with that later.

"You said you hadn't found any other mention of the story when you searched the library," he went on.

"No, nothing."

Peter spread his hands. "I rest my case."

"Meaning that the only reason it's printed in the clan chronicle is that Burke put it there."

"You have to admit it fits."

"Yes. It fits." Athena leaned back again. "What this boils down to, Peter, is that Christopher and I are even again. Now that you've disproved his evidence, neither of us has the least bit of proof to substantiate our version of what happened that night."

"But you just said Angus didn't sign over the deed until six weeks after Christmas, Athena. Surely that negates the theory that he lost it in a game of chance."

"My father always maintained that Angus MacKay was coerced into signing over the deed. It's a rather ghastly thought, isn't it?"

"I wouldn't say any of this business is very pretty. What happened 350 years ago is bad enough. But what Burke is doing to you now—" The stricken expression on her face stopped him. He studied her carefully over the candlelight. "You care very much for him, don't you, Athena?"

Despite herself, she had to laugh. "I must wear my heart on my sleeve. You're the second person to ask me that question."

Peter reached for her hands. He noticed they were cold. He massaged them gently as he spoke. "Then it must be true. I can't say I'm happy to hear it, but . . ." He sighed, then smiled at her. "All right, on to more practical matters. What's your next move in this crazy game?"

"I have to confront Christopher with what information I have—inconclusive as it is. I have to get him to stop work at Kildrurry. Then, I have five more days to find proof that Angus MacKay did not sign that deed over of his own volition."

"And what if you can't convince him?"

She took a deep breath. "I'm not sure. I thought . . . I thought he was an honorable man. Now . . ." Athena shook her head. "I just don't know."

He leaned over, squeezing her hands reassuringly. "I want you to promise me something, Athena. When this is over—no matter what happens—I want you to think about coming to London. I think the research we're doing there is important, perhaps the most important to be done in psychic research in years. Some of it should fit in very well with your own work. I want to share it with you. I want you to be part of the breakthrough."

She started to speak, but he interrupted her. "No, don't give me your answer now. I only ask that you think about it." He gave her hand a final squeeze. "Okay?"

Athena smiled, nodding. "All right, Peter. I'll think about it. I promise."

Clouds passed over the moon, bathing the castle in sporadic patterns of light and dark. Its towers were silhouetted eerily against the sky. Athena thought that tonight Burke House looked particularly mysterious and formidable.

"It's right out of an old horror movie," Peter commented, pulling his car to a stop. He walked her to the door. "This gargoyle's a nice touch. Pleasant-looking fellow."

Athena looked at the grotesque creature and laughed. "That's what I said the day I arrived here." She opened the door. "You have to admit he adds atmosphere."

"As if Burke House needs it." Peter shivered, standing in the doorway. "This place gives me the creeps. How can you stand to stay here?"

"It's worse at night," she told him. "By day it can be charming, like a page from the past."

"Or the aftermath of a bad nightmare." He took her gently by the shoulders. "You'll remember what I said, won't you, Athena? London is beautiful this time of year."

"I'll remember, Peter," she answered softly. "And thank you. For everything."

It seemed perfectly natural that Peter should give her a quick kiss good-night. The light touch of his lips on her mouth was warm and companionable, like his personality. It was pleasant in his arms. She found none of the danger and excitement that was always present with Christopher; but it was comfortable. Tonight that was what she needed.

After he left she closed the door and tried to make her way through the hallway to the stairs without a light. When it went on unexpectedly, she gave a startled gasp.

"That was a touching little scene. You don't waste time, do you, Athena?"

"Christopher!" He was standing outside the library door, a half-consumed drink in his hand. He was wearing a smoke-gray suit, and she saw fire in his eyes beneath the icy calmness. Despite the innocence of the scene with Peter a moment ago, Athena flushed with embarrassment, realizing how it could be misconstrued. Her own anger with him was temporarily forgotten. "You weren't supposed to be home until tomorrow."

"I changed my plans." He glanced upstairs, then back to her. "I'd like to talk to you. In the library."

"Christopher, it's late. I—"

"Now!"

Athena stared at him for a moment, remembering in vivid detail what she had seen that day at Kildrurry. The hurt of his betrayal was brutally fresh. She would confront him on her own terms and at her own time. "No." She spoke evenly despite her pounding heart. "I'll see you tomorrow."

She had taken only two steps before he grabbed her arm, propelling her into the library. "We'll talk right now," he said, pushing her into a chair. "I want to know what the hell were you doing out with that man?"

"Peter Scott," Athena corrected automatically. He was pacing in front of the fire. He reminded her of a wild animal—stalking, waiting to lash out. He wasn't just angry, she realized with a flicker of panic, he was furious. She felt her own temper rise and controlled it. This was not the time to challenge him about Kildrurry. "We had dinner together," she said calmly.

"How nice for you both." His tone was contemptuous. "And that little scene at the door? Was that payment for your portion of the bill? And London? Is that to be the tip?"

Athena's eyes locked on his. She felt a pressure building behind her eyes but refused to acknowledge it. She fought to keep her voice even. "You're talking nonsense. Peter merely offered to show me the work he's doing in London. I haven't given him my answer."

"No, but you're thinking about it."

"It might be a good career move after I leave here."

"Ah, yes," he said, his voice full of scorn. "Your career. That means a lot to you, doesn't it, Athena?"

"Of course it does." Where's he leading? she wondered, feeling the small hairs rise on the back of her neck. "My work has always been important to me," she told him guardedly. "I've never suggested otherwise."

"No. On that score, at least, you've been honest."

"What's that supposed to mean?"

"It means that I've been a fool, Athena." He stopped pacing to stand in front of her. He rose up before her like a modern-day Hercules. The fire behind him was a fitting backdrop to his fury and unconsciously, she drew in her breath. "I was beginning to believe we shared something," he went on. "I was gullible enough to think I meant more to you than just the key to Kildrurry."

"But, I—"

"No," he broke in. "Let me finish." He moved closer to her and she shrank back in her seat. "That was the plan, wasn't it? Get what you want, then run off with the first promising male. Even better if he could help you along in your career." He moved restlessly. "And I bought it. I knew better and yet I bought the whole damn parcel of lies!"

"Lies!" Something snapped inside Athena, and she no longer cared how angry he was or how dangerous. She exploded out of her chair, furious. "How dare you! After what you've done you've got one hell of a nerve accusing *me* of lying!"

"I'm merely calling it as I see it," he said with infuriating calm. "If you can't stand losing, don't play the game."

"Or don't play with cheaters!" she blazed.

His face darkened. "I don't like to be called names, Athena."

"No? Sorry, I was just calling it as I see it," she said, twisting his words and hurling them back at him.

"Athena, what are you talking about?"

"Don't tell me you've forgotten already? What a convenient memory you have. Or is it just that Kildrurry means so little to you?"

"What in hell does Kildrurry have to do with this?"

"About half a million pounds, I'd say, at a rough guess. Perhaps more. Not every golf course comes complete with its own ghost."

"I told you we'd discuss the damn golf course at the end of the week. *If* you're still here."

"Don't give me that bull, Christopher! I may be gullible, but even I know when I've been had. By then there won't be anything left to discuss." There was a catch in her throat. "Hasn't this past week meant anything to you?" She was looking up at him, her hazel eyes huge with pain. She hadn't meant to say it. She wanted to take refuge in her anger, to concentrate on that, not the pain.

"It's meant everything you intended it to," he retorted angrily. "What do you want from me, Athena? A pat on the back for playing your part so well?"

"I haven't been playing a part, dammit! Will you stop saying that!" He could see her tremble with the sobs she was fighting to control. "You're the one who's been unscrupulous."

Firmly Christopher clamped down on his anger. "Will you try to make sense? You're talking in riddles."

"Sorry." Athena took another moment to get herself in hand. "I'll try to make it easier for you to understand. You agreed to give me three weeks to find proof that Kildrurry belongs to the MacKays. Then, while you lured me to your bed, you went full speed ahead with your plans without the slightest pang of conscience."

Christopher towered over her, but she was too angry to notice. "I think you've got that a bit turned around, Athena. If anyone was doing the luring, it was you. You're the one who had everything to gain by stalling for time."

She stared at him, aghast. "Stalling for time! Is that why you think I went to bed with you? You think I'd actually sell my body to gain a little time?"

"I don't know what you might do to get Kildrurry." His eyes narrowed as he studied her defiant face. "You're obsessed by it."

"I'm determined to see justice done. And if that's an obsession, then I'm guilty. At least I haven't used you! I haven't caressed you with one hand while stabbing you in the back with the other!''

"You're free with your accusations, Athena," he said with deadly calm. "Just what am I supposed to have done?"

"Christopher, how far are you prepared to carry this thing? You know damn well what you've done. You couldn't wait five days. Five lousy days! Not even to honor a promise."

His hand closed on her wrist and there was a hard gleam in his eyes. "I haven't broken any promises to you," he said in a low voice.

"No? Then I guess I must have imagined that bulldozer at Kildrurry today." She went on recklessly, ignoring the pressure of his fingers on her arms. "Or the surveyors, or the construction workers."

"What are you talking about? There's no construction going on at Kildrurry."

She heard the ring of truth in his denial, but was too angry and hurt to heed it. "Are you calling me a liar, Christopher? I saw them with my own eyes. Today—when I came back from Edinburgh."

Christopher muttered a short expletive and released her arm. Athena watched in stunned silence as he stormed out of the library and into the hall. She heard him pick up the phone and dial a number.

"Christopher, it's one o'clock in the morning," she said, following him.

He looked at her but said nothing as he stood with the receiver in his hand, waiting. After another moment or two she heard the muffled sound of a man's voice on the other end of the line.

"Begley? Burke here." She heard more muted sounds, then Christopher boomed, "I don't give a damn what time it is. What the hell is going on at Kildrurry? I told you Saturday night to hold off work there until I gave the word.''

Athena heard a loud protest from the other end, then Christopher's angry retort. "That's *his* problem. If he can't wait until we're ready he can bloody well get out of the deal. I want those men and their machines out of there first thing tomorrow morning!''

He slammed down the receiver and turned back to her. "Begley overstepped his authority,'' he told her tightly. "One of our backers threatened to renege on the deal if we didn't start work on the golf course immediately. He'll be taken care of tomorrow.'' He met her eyes. "I had no idea about this, Athena. You have until the end of the week to complete your work. *As I promised.*''

Without waiting for an answer, he turned and walked back into the library. Athena followed him. He was facing the fire, his back turned to her.

"William telephoned yesterday,'' she told him. "I left a message for you at your office. He must have been—he must have wanted to speak to you about the golf course. He seemed very upset you weren't here.''

Christopher didn't answer. He didn't even acknowledge her presence in the room. One of his arms rested on the fireplace mantel. His back was rigid. "I thought you should know,'' she went on quietly. "I don't want you to be too hard on him. I don't think he realized—I don't think he understood our agreement.''

She might have been talking to a statue. He didn't move. He didn't speak. He just continued to stare into the fire. She walked up behind him and placed a tentative hand on his arm. She felt him flinch and quickly dropped her hand to her side.

"Christopher, I'm sorry. I should have known you wouldn't betray me like that." Still he didn't move, and his silence cut through her heart like a knife. She searched for the words to reach him. "I should have trusted you. I know that now."

Then he looked at her, and when she saw his face she shrank back. There was no more anger left in his eyes. Instead there was a terrible, gaping emptiness. Athena could find no emotion of any kind. No anger, no hurt, just a numbness, which in its way was far more devastating to her than his anger had ever been.

"What do you want from me, Athena?" he asked her for the second time that night. His expressionless voice was like ice. She wanted to reach out to him, but she was afraid she would only be rejected again. He was closing her out, just as surely as if he'd slammed a door in her face.

His fingers tightened on the mantel. He wanted her so much in that moment but he was afraid if he didn't hold on he might reach out and hurt her. When he'd come home earlier to find she'd gone out with Scott, he'd been driven half out of his mind. Christopher recognized the emotion for what it was. And he hated himself for it.

Fury at his lack of control made him speak even more harshly. "I said what do you want, dammit?"

"I want *you*," she said softly. "But I think I'm asking for more than you can give." Athena had to concentrate on what she was saying. She didn't want to be led astray by her need to touch him, to love him. She couldn't break down! "On our way back from Edinburgh, you asked me to trust you. I wasn't ready then. I was confused. In many ways I still am. There's so much that's still not resolved between us. So many things we're unable to say or share."

Athena stopped. She was expressing herself badly. Why were the important things so difficult to put into words?

"When I saw them working at Kildrurry today, I wanted to believe it was a mistake—that you hadn't betrayed me. But the evidence was there, before my eyes. I . . . I didn't know what else to believe."

She waited, but he said nothing. "You're not making this easy for me, are you?"

"Why should I?"

Athena felt a surge of aggravation. "Good God, Christopher! I'm trying to apologize."

"I hear you, Athena." She could see he was struggling for control. She saw anger breaking through the void and was glad. Rage was preferable to the terrible curtain he could draw over his feelings. "You don't owe me an apology." He studied the whisky in his glass. "I understand about Kildrurry." His eyes lifted to her, and she saw the familiar lines of bitterness around his mouth. "I understand more about you than you think."

"Do you, Christopher? Then why can't you be open with me? Why can't you let me in?"

"Why? So it'll be easier to manipulate me to get what you want?" He drained his drink, then crossed to the bar to pour another. Why couldn't she drop the subject? Why did she have to stand there and make him want her when he should be forgetting?

"I haven't manipulated you!"

His fingers tightened around the glass. "Forget it, will you, Athena?" He took a long swallow of his drink. "What you do with your life is your business."

Athena felt hot tears burning behind her eyes. She took a deep breath. She would not let herself break down. "Christopher, this is important." When he turned away she flew at him with a cry of frustration. "Why won't you listen to me?"

Abruptly he put down his glass and dragged her into his arms. "Why can't you let it go, Athena? It would be so much better—for both of us—if you'd finish your work and leave."

She raised her head to him. "Is that what you want me to do?" Her voice was a strangled whisper and her eyes bored into his. "Tell me the truth, Christopher, because if you want me to leave I swear I'll be out of here by tomorrow morning."

He wanted to tell her yes—yes, leave. If she was gone, his life would be his own again. He would stop being driven—he would be back in control. But even as these thoughts ran through his mind, he was distracted by the way he knew she would taste if he reached down right now and kissed her and by his never-ending desire for her.

"No," he whispered. "I don't want you to go. I need you. Dammit, Athena, I need you!"

Nine

His mouth was on hers, rough and desperate. He could feel the anger pouring out of him, directed at her, punishing her for changing his life so that it would never again be the same. "I wanted to possess you. But it's you who've possessed me!"

He ravished her lips as if he couldn't get enough of them. One hand crushed her into his body where she felt the fierce pounding of his heart. The other tangled in her hair to pull her head up to receive his kiss. Hungrily his lips touched her hair, her eyes, her ears, finally coming back to feast on her mouth as if he would devour it.

Athena shivered against him, her body throbbing with longing. Only the realization that he was holding part of himself back made her hesitate. She wanted more than just a physical union; she wanted him to share his mind and spirit, his fears as well as his joys. She wanted the bond between them to be complete.

Standing on the tips of her toes, she lifted her arms t circle his neck. She felt the hard muscles ripple beneath he touch. His skin was warm from the fire, his scent fresh an musky. "Christopher." His name was a soft sigh agains his chest. "I don't know if this is right, but it's the onl way you'll let me in. And, God help me, I need you, too!"

He looked down at her and his expression was smolder ing. The desire in his eyes mingled with primitive mal satisfaction. An emotional storm was building inside him and he knew that soon it would be out of his control. H triumphed in the power of the kiss as he ached from th feel of her pliant body pressed into his. He molded her t him, his fingers gripping the soft, yielding flesh of he buttocks. He was wild with the desire to have her, to tak her here and now and then be finally, mercifully, free.

The fierceness of his need drove them both. He wa pulling at her blouse, having no patience for the button She heard several of them pop across the room, then fe the sharp rip of silk, but she was beyond caring. All tha mattered was the touch of his hands on her skin, the won derful crush of his flesh against hers. She felt her bra an skirt fall to the floor without quite knowing how he ha managed it. Then she was completely naked and his hand were everywhere, too driven now to linger in any one spo for more than a second, needing to seek out each warm secret place on her body. She gasped softly and twine desperate fingers into his hair, shuddering beneath th sudden rush of sensations that were bombarding he senses.

"Yes," he said huskily, inflamed by her response. "M God, Athena. *Yes!*"

She fumbled with his clothes, then somehow they wer off. She sighed as her fingers spread across the bunchin muscles she loved, the human steel that moved an strained beneath her touch. His mouth crushed hers as he pulled her to the floor. Hazily Athena felt the sensuous softness of the sealskin rug beneath her skin, and then his weight was on her and she felt nothing else.

One large, powerful hand encircled a breast and Athena trembled violently. She was hot with desire, intoxicated with the feel of him. His tongue plunged deep into her mouth and she squirmed beneath him, arching upward, the driving ache inside her screaming for satisfaction. Then his teeth and tongue were on her breast, and she thought she would surely go out of her mind.

Christopher felt the hammering of her heart and knew it matched his own. Her hands urged him on, her soft moans acted as an aphrodisiac to his already faltering control. She moved urgently beneath him, and he was driven to the breaking point. Slipping his fingers inside her, he found her soft, moist and ready for him. The fragile thread was broken. With a shattered moan, he felt himself hurled beyond the line of reason.

He entered her with a desperation that left them both reeling. The climax came almost instantly—a dizzying, hurtling explosion. Athena clutched him, gasping for breath as he pulled her up and over the peak with him. Together they sought and found their moment. And then they were still.

His face was buried in her shoulder, and she could hear his ragged breaths in the aftermath of spent passion. Although he was still on top of her, he had shifted his weight so that she was not uncomfortable. His body was warm and damp and she loved the sensation of it against her. She smiled, feeling deliciously, totally at peace.

He was the first to move, raising up on one elbow to study her in the firelight. Her skin still glowed from their lovemaking, and her eyes were half-closed and misty with fulfillment. Her hair was a deep, russet brown and curls spilled about her milky-white shoulders, and Christopher thought she had never looked more enticing.

"You're staring," she said, smiling lazily. Every muscle and bone in her body was relaxed. Athena felt as if she were floating blissfully in a luxurious stream of contentment.

"You've enchanted me." His deep voice was like the touch of velvet on her naked skin. She felt a brief flicker of arousal and smiled.

"No," she murmured. Her eyes were unbelievably heavy and she closed them. "It's you. You're the one who's cast the spell."

She felt him move away from her, and without opening her eyes, reached out to stop him. "No," she murmured. "Don't go. I want to stay like this forever."

He sat back on his heels and looked at her lying naked on the rug, her body soft, ripe and eminently desirable. Christopher felt a sharp shaft of passion and was surprised. Why, of all the women he had ever known, did this one have such a devastating effect on him? Even when he was fresh from loving her, she had him wanting her all over again.

"You'd make a pretty picture in the morning when Lachlan came in to build up the fire," he told her, reaching for their clothing.

Athena chuckled softly, imagining the dour butler's reaction. "He'd be scandalized." Her chuckle developed into a low, throaty laugh. "It might be worth it just to get some kind of rise out of him. I think he's half-robot."

"That kind of excitement I can do without," he said dryly. "He'd probably give his notice on the spot." He finished picking up their clothes, then grinned mischie-

vously. "On the other hand, he might just drop pok
tongs and ravish you on the spot."

She sat up at this. *"Lachlan!"*

His eyes skimmed her body. "You do have an extraordinary effect on the male libido, Athena."

Before she could answer, he stooped down and lifted her into his arms. Her hair floated about her head to tickle his arms. He felt his body hardening again and silently cursed. She had too much effect on *his* libido, he thought. He was going to have to deal with that. But not tonight. Tonight he would get his fill of her.

"Where are you carrying me off to, oh Viking warrior?" she teased. Athena loved the feel of his body against hers as he transported her effortlessly up the stairs.

"To my lair, fair maiden," he answered, giving in to the urge to nuzzle one tantalizing breast. "There, the better to ravish you!"

It was not until the following evening that Athena had an opportunity to speak to Christopher about her discovery at the records office. He'd already left for the office when she awakened that morning, and the night before had been too filled with love to think about ghosts.

After Gram retired to her room, Athena suggested that they take a drive. "I think better when I'm out of here," she told him. "Burke House is too filled with the past. I know you think it's crazy, but I can feel it. I sense it all around me. I'll be able to put things in better perspective if we go somewhere else."

Christopher followed the winding course of the mountain, stopping at a cliff turnout that commanded a spectacular view of the ocean. The last glow of day had already faded from the evening sky, and darkness was rapidly blanketing the unruly sea.

"It seems more treacherous at night, doesn't it?" she said, listening to the steady slap of the waves on the cliff below them.

"It's treacherous all the time," he answered quietly. "Too many men have made the mistake of underestimating its power. The North Sea is mercurial and unforgiving."

"You sound as if you speak from experience."

"My father drowned out there." His voice was flat, unemotional.

Athena's eyes flew to him. Megan hadn't told her about this. Perhaps she thought it was common knowledge. He was sitting impassively, staring out to sea, his profile seemingly chiseled from granite. "How did it happen?" she asked softly.

"We had a boat—a thirty-foot sloop. The *Mary B.* My brother and I sometimes raced her." He spoke without turning his head, his tone matter-of-fact, as if he had long since come to terms with the tragedy. "Late one afternoon, my father took the *Mary B.* out alone. There had been storm warnings all day. He never came back. They found the sloop the following afternoon, smashed against the cliffs. There was no sign of my father's body."

"If there were storm warnings, why did he go out? Didn't he know?"

"He knew. My father loved the sea. He was a seasoned sailor. He would have known."

"Then why—"

"Because he was tired of living." He looked at her. "He had lost interest in life years before."

"When your mother left," she filled in quietly.

She caught his quick look of surprise. A shadow crossed his face and she thought he was going to share something with her, then the moment passed and he went on. "He never got over her going. For a while he tried to bury the pain in his work, but eventually even that wasn't enough. He was ready to go. That night I think he simply chose his own time and his own place.''

Neither of them spoke for several minutes. Another clue to the enigmatic Christopher Burke clicked into her head. His mother, his father, his wife and with her, his brother. More than enough heartache for several lifetimes. And he had closed it all up inside. ''I'm sorry,'' she said simply, unable to put her emotions into words.

''I tried to be, but I couldn't. My father had the right to find his own kind of peace.''

''Perhaps,'' she said doubtfully. ''But I'm not sure anyone has the right to leave behind the wreckage of other people's lives. He had a commitment, a responsibility—to you and your brother. And even to Gram.''

''And what about his responsibility to himself?''

''I believe in that, too. But not at the expense of others.'' The darkness around them was complete, and she could just make out his imposing form across the seat from her. Somehow the lack of light made it more intimate. She found it easier to share her thoughts and emotions. ''With freedom has to come responsibility—I think perhaps in equal proportions. One without the other creates an imbalance in life.''

''Do you always honor your responsibilities, Athena?'' Although she couldn't see his face clearly, she picked up the new, sharper edge to his voice. He's testing me, she realized.

''I try to, Christopher. I don't always succeed. But I try.''

''Do you, Athena?'' His voice was thoughtful. ''I wonder which you would choose if it meant something you really wanted—say Kildrurry? Perhaps you might be torn by prior responsibilities, by other commitments.''

She worked to control a brief flicker of temper. ''You still insist I came here to finagle Kildrurry back at any cost.''

''The thought does recur periodically.''

''Why!'' she demanded. ''Just when I think we're coming closer together, you rake all that up again. What does it take to convince you? Why are you so stubborn?''

''Not stubborn, Athena. Realistic.'' She could hear the anger building in him and wanted to reach out and stop it, now, before they were arguing again. There was too little time left for fighting. ''You and your family have been obsessed with that damn castle for years.''

''Yes, I want Kildrurry,'' she protested. ''And I'm prepared to go to any legal lengths to get it back. But that's the extent of what I'm willing to do. I won't resort to subterfuge. And I certainly won't use myself as bait.''

''And what happens when you fail?''

The condescending tone was back in his voice and she wanted to scream. ''I won't fail. As a matter of fact, I'm on the brink of succeeding!'' Athena stopped, dismayed at her lack of control. This wasn't the way she'd planned to tell him. The reason for getting out of the house was to talk quietly, intimately. Now she was yelling at him and he was glaring back at her from across the seat. ''I'm sorry. We certainly know how to push each other's buttons, don't we?''

''Among other things. There are some buttons we push with rather amazing results.'' He moved in the darkness, and she knew he had turned to her. ''We drove out here for a reason, Athena,'' he said, his voice quiet now. ''Why don't you tell me what's on your mind.''

She recognized his attempt at peacemaking and accepted it gratefully. "I've already stuck my foot in it," she said ruefully. "I might as well tell you the rest."

Trying to keep it simple, Athena told him about finding the deed at the records office, then went on to share her suspicions about how the "gambling" version of the MacKay-Burke feud happened to find its way into the clan chronicle. She felt him stiffen when she mentioned her dinner with Peter, but decided he would have to know her source sooner or later. When she was finished, he sat in stunned silence.

"You really have been busy, haven't you?" Since the question was clearly rhetorical, Athena kept quiet while he collected his thoughts. "It seems I owe you a very large apology," he said at length. "About 350 years' worth of apology."

"I haven't proved anything yet," she reminded him. "All I know is that Angus MacKay signed the deed over six weeks after he was supposed to have died. I want to know what happened to him during that time."

"You don't have to prove anything, Athena. The date on the deed is sufficient." She could hear the weariness in his voice. He's sick of this whole business, she thought. In a way, it's plagued his life nearly as much as it has mine. But I can't let go of it yet. Dad would never want me to accept Kildrurry unless I was sure it belonged to the MacKays.

"I have to know the truth, Christopher," she told him. "I have to know what happened."

"And you call me stubborn." He moved closer to her, letting his hand rest lightly on her shoulder. Absently he touched a curl. "All right. Where do we go from here?"

"*We?*"

"I'd say the least I can do is help you find your proof. Where do we start?"

She looked at him and smiled. "I was hoping you'd feel that way. I think I'm going to need all the help I can get."

"That sounds ominous," he said, laughing. "Maybe I volunteered too quickly. Just what *do* you have in mind?"

"I've decided to assume that my father's version of the story is the correct one. He maintained that Angus was captured that Christmas Eve and tortured until he signed over the clan holdings."

"Pleasant thought."

"I know, but right now it's the likeliest explanation." She paused. "Does Burke House have any dungeons?"

"Good Lord, your mind is running along sinister lines. I seem to remember an old tower room was used for that purpose. But it was destroyed in a raid before the sixteenth century, so it would have been before Angus's time."

She surprised him by looking pleased. "Good. I was sure that wasn't where he was kept anyway."

"How did you arrive at that remarkable conclusion?"

"Because Angus's ghost haunts outside Gram's room." Anticipating his objection, she cut him off. "Wait a minute. I know what you think of all that, but the fact remains that most restless 'spirits' relive the final traumatic moments of their lives. They continually repeat the same pattern. The hallway leading up to Gram's room must have special significance to Angus."

"Your logic is fascinating."

"You'll have to admit it's as good a place to start as any." She looked at him through the darkness. "How's about it, Christopher? Are you with me or not?"

"Oh, I'm with you, of course," he said, barely disguising the laughter in his voice. "With that kind of deductive reasoning, how can we fail?"

They began their search in the morning. At Christopher's insistence, they started at the end of the hallway farthest from Gram's room. "There's no sense disturbing her until we know we're onto something," he told her.

His plan worked for about fifteen minutes. At the end of that time, Gram came wheeling out of her room demanding to know "who was raisin' all the ruckus." After that, and over Christopher's strenuous objections, she became a working member of the operation. Ordering a small hammer from Lachlan, she tapped her own path along the hallway beside Athena and her grandson. Sneaking looks at her now and then, Athena thought the old woman was having the time of her life. By the end of the day, she only wished she could share some of Gram's exuberance.

"I'm not sure my arms will ever be the same," she complained, rubbing them gingerly as she and Christopher relaxed in the library. "Why is it your muscles don't ache?"

"Ah, you've unearthed my secret," he said with a wink. "In my spare time I hire myself out to find secret passages and burial chambers. The Egyptians love my work."

"Be serious, Christopher," she said wearily. "I'm beginning to feel foolish going from room to room poking on walls. I caught Lachlan peeking around the corner at us this afternoon. He looked as if he were going to cry."

"Lachlan finds Mickey Mouse depressing. We've only been at it one day, Athena. Give it some time."

They began again early the next morning. Since Christopher had to work during the afternoon, Athena was determined to cover as much ground as possible before he left. By now Fiona had volunteered to help, and the four of them made good progress down the corridor. Toward the end of the morning, there was only Gram's room left.

"If there was a secret room in here I'd know about it," Gram protested. "I don't care to have people pokin' about in me room."

"We've tried every other wall in this wing," Athena told her. "This is our last hope."

"Maybe," the old woman said doubtfully. "Still, I don't like the idea that the old bounder might have been sharin' me room with me all these years."

Ironically, in the end it was Gram who made the discovery. Working lower than the others because of her wheelchair, she was pounding lightly on the wall to the right of her fireplace when the sound took on a hollow tone. Stopping, she tried tapping again with the same results.

"Oh, oh. What do we have here?" The old woman turned to Athena. "You'd better have a look at this, lass. Either my ears are worse than I thought, or this bit of wall sounds different from the rest."

Athena hurried over, hardly daring to hope that Gram had stumbled onto something. Holding her breath, she knocked gently against the wall. She stopped and tried a little bit to the right, and then to the left. It did sound hollow!

Even as she poked and prodded, she reminded herself that given the religious climate of the sixteenth century, secret rooms, or priest's holes, were not uncommon in Britain. Even if this was a hideaway, there was no guarantee it had ever been used for Angus MacKay.

Yet the more she knocked and tapped, the more the fine hairs rose on the back of her neck. This was it, she told herself. This was what they had been looking for!

"If there's a secret room in here, this would be the logical place to put it," Christopher said, examining the wall. "This part of the room, or more particularly the fireplace, backs onto the stairway. All the builder had to do was utilize the dead space to either side of the flue."

"And it would also allow exit to the outside," Athena added, her excitement growing. "Come on, everyone. Let's start at the top and work our way down systematically. There has to be a controlling mechanism somewhere."

This time it was Christopher who found the secret. Underneath the carved fireplace mantel, running along the inside top of the opening, was a row of tiny decorative balls. Examining each one in turn, he found one of them to be loose. When he turned it, there was a loud grating noise and a three-foot-square section of the wall popped open.

"Christopher, you did it!" Athena cried, throwing her arms around him.

"Who would have thought it?" Gram said, eyeing the wall in astonishment. "Now what's inside that filthy hole? That's what I want to know."

Christopher was already at work on the answer to her question. When it popped open, the door only moved an inch or two from the wall. "It's stuck," he announced. "God knows how long it's been since it was last opened. I'm going to have to pry it out."

Using the fireplace poker as a wedge, he gradually worked the door out until there was a six-inch opening. Then, placing his back against the wall for leverage, he used his hands and feet to force it open the rest of the way.

"It's built with butt hinges," he told them, examining the inside of the trap door. "They're so old they've become rusted and fused together in places. No wonder it was so hard to budge."

He stepped back and looked at Athena. "I think you should be the first to look inside."

Despite her excitement, Athena held back for a moment. What if the room's empty? she thought. What if we've gone through all this for nothing? She caught Christopher's eye and he winked encouragingly. She smiled and took a tentative step forward. The light from Gram's window was spilling over into the opening, but the interior was still very dim. Taking a deep breath, she walked over and looked inside.

The room was tiny—Athena estimated about three feet deep by four feet wide—and it smelled very stale and musty. The back of the chamber was the same depth as the fireplace, cleverly concealing it, as Christopher guessed, from inquisitive eyes. When she was better adjusted to the dim light, she saw that there was another door leading out of the room off to one side. That would be the outside exit, she thought, a quick, effective escape to the outside world in case of invasion or religious persecution.

The next thing she saw made her heart beat faster; it was a large metal ring attached to the back wall. From this ring hung two old, very rusty chains. Slowly her eyes ran down the length of the chains to the floor. "Oh my God!" She jerked backward into the room.

"Athena, what is it?" Her face was completely drained of color, and when Christopher put his arms around her shoulders, they were trembling violently. "Are you all right?"

She nodded. "I'm fine. It was just a shock." Slowly, reluctantly, she walked back to the hidden room and pointed. "Look—down there, beside the chains."

When neither of them spoke for several minutes, Gram exploded. "Well, what is it? Don't just stand there, you two. What's in there?"

Athena turned to Gram, her voice starkly quiet. "I think we've found him, Gram. I think we've found what's left of Angus MacKay."

"Just the thought of that poor man being chained in that—that hole for six weeks turns my blood to ice. He wouldn't have been able to stand upright or even stretch out his legs." Athena shuddered. "He must have suffered horribly."

They were huddled together in the library. Much to Lachlan's gloomy disapproval, Fiona had been included. He had made them substantial hot toddies to which Athena suspected more than a wee dram had been added. Before them on the table, in pathetic array, were the last personal effects of Angus MacKay.

"He was a tough old codger, no doubt about it," Gram pronounced with reluctant admiration. "Imagin' goin' through all that before signin' over the deed." She shook her small head. "And to think he was there all the time— in me own room!"

"Did you really see his bones?" Fiona asked in a small voice. Of the four, she alone had declined to look into the priest's hole, claiming she wouldn't sleep another wink for the rest of her life if she did. Now that the initial shock was wearing off, however, her natural curiosity was coming to the fore.

"Enough to recognize that it was, *had been* a man," Athena said with a little shudder.

"But—but how could you tell it was him? Angus, I mean?" Fiona persisted in a small voice.

"Considering the legend, there wasn't much doubt even if we hadn't found his knife and buckle on the floor." Christopher nodded to the table. "They're rusty, but you can just make out his initials. And the buckle has the crude outline of a bow with a single vertical line through it, which was one of the earliest Clan MacKay symbols."

"You did it, lass," Gram said with satisfaction. "Aye, just as I knew you would."

"She's right, Athena," Christopher told her. "You can finally rest your case. And you can take Kildrurry. Legally, and in every other sense, it's yours."

"I wish Dad could hear that."

Christopher watched her and realized how much her father had meant to her. "Maybe he can," he said softly. "Aren't you the one who said anything was possible?"

She looked at him for a long moment, then smiled, grateful to him for understanding.

"You've got his persistence," he went on, remembering the years of letters, appeals and threats from the Clan MacKay. He laughed softly. "He must have been quite a man. But it's paid off. You have Kildrurry and you've even laid old Angus to rest."

"Actually," she began, looking at him over her toddy, "we haven't."

"Haven't what?"

"Haven't laid his spirit to rest."

He looked at her as if she was joking. "You've found the deed, and you've found Angus. You can even give his remains a proper burial if you want. What else can you do?"

"We can have a séance."

"A séance." He leaned forward in his chair, his voice incredulous. "A *séance*!"

"We have to, Christopher. If we don't, Angus won't know that it's all right for him to leave."

"Leave! Of course he's going to leave. I'm going to carry his bones out of here myself."

"I mean his spirit—the part of him that walks the halls at night terrifying Gram." He was looking at her as if she'd gone completely potty. "Don't you see, you have to tell him it's all right now, that you've given Kildrurry back—that he can go peacefully to his rest."

"*I* have to tell him? Why me, of all people?"

"It has to be you because you're the master of Burke House, the rightful descendant of the Burke who did him the injustice." She smiled, wishing he'd stop looking at her like that. "It's easy, really. And it will only take a few minutes."

"And when do you plan to hold this—this séance of yours?"

"Tonight would be nice," she said in a small voice. "There's no time like the present, they say."

"Tonight," he repeated flatly. "And I have to be there."

"You more than anyone else." She went over and sat on the arm of his chair. "Think of all he went through, Christopher. This is the least you can do for him."

Christopher looked at her, then shook his head. "I don't believe it. I simply don't believe it. How do you talk me into these things?"

When Fiona heard that the séance was to be held in Gram's room, she quickly excused herself from the proceedings. Athena offered the same option to Gram but the old lady laughed and said she wouldn't miss the "doin's" for the world.

Christopher had already moved Angus's remains to a downstairs room. Tomorrow he would call the authorities and inform them of their discovery and his plans to dispose of the bones. Although they knew the "hole" was empty, each of them continued to feel Angus's presence in the room. Athena, who was most affected, claimed it would aid them in making contact. This caused Gram to clap her hands in excitement and Christopher to raise his eyes to the ceiling in long-suffering silence.

"We'll wait until just before midnight," she told them. "That's when I usually observe the phenomenon. We can sit comfortably at the table here. Gram needn't move from her wheelchair."

"Do we hold hands?" Christopher asked dryly.

"I don't think that will be necessary. In this case we just want to give him a message. We're not going to attempt to raise any other spirits."

"Thank God for small favors," he murmured. "And just what is my role in all this? You'd better give me my lines."

"It doesn't have to be rehearsed. Just say you've made restitution for the injustices done to him and that it's all right for him to go on to the next astral plane."

"Astral plane," he repeated. "I really have to say that."

She smiled at him. "It would help."

"By all means. Anything to help." He sat down in front of the table. "All right," he pronounced. "I'm ready. Bring on the ghost."

Ten

―――――

Are you asleep?"

"No," he grumbled. "It's difficult to sleep when you've just made a complete idiot of yourself."

She turned over to snuggle against him. "Don't be silly. You were wonderful. You'd make a great medium."

He laughed. "God forbid." He moved his arms around her until her body was cradled into his. He could feel the steady beat of her heart and was content. "What makes you think he heard? Assuming, of course, there was anyone there to listen."

"He heard," she told him confidently. "Angus was there. He heard you."

"Ah, to have your faith." Absently he twirled one of her curls around his finger. "I'm glad we moved Gram across the hall for tonight. I expected her to be exhausted after all the excitement, yet she looked as if she were ready to take on a whole house of horrors. It's remarkable.''

"She's finally free of her old nemesis. It seems to have given her a new zest for life."

"She is happier now, but I'm damned if I'll give the credit to a ghost. You're the one who's made the difference." He ran his hand softly along her cheek, wondering at the sunshine she had brought into his home, into his life. Everywhere she went lights seemed to go on. It was easy to laugh around Athena. She cared, and she had a way of making others care, too. "You've made her feel special and needed again," he went on quietly. "I'd forgotten how important that can be for someone her age."

"For everyone, Christopher. It's important for everyone."

"Yes," he said thoughtfully. "I suppose it is."

Athena wriggled against him contentedly. "It's been a long day."

"That's something of an understatement. I've hunted for secret rooms, helped solve a 350-year-old murder mystery and exorcised a ghost." He chuckled softly. "It's been a very busy day."

"Think of how boring it's going to be from now on with no Angus to liven up the nights."

"I can do with a little boredom for a change. I haven't had a quiet moment since you arrived."

She turned and nibbled lightly at his ear. "Are you complaining?"

Christopher felt the sudden, sharp stab of arousal he was coming to associate with her. "No, I'm not complaining," he said, burying his lips in her hair.

Athena wondered if she would ever meet another man who could stir her this way. She raised up on one elbow and studied him in the moonlight.

"Oh-oh," he said, catching the gleam in her eyes. "Whenever you get that look on your face you're cooking up something. And it usually involves me."

She ran the tip of her finger over the strong lines of his cheek and said, "I think you'll approve of what I have in mind." Tilting her face, she kissed him softly on the lips. "It's an activity at which you're particularly adept."

His hand slipped beneath her nightgown and she gave a pleasurable little gasp. "Oh, and just what sort of activity is that?" He eased the gown over her head, then ran his hands down the smooth length of her body. "Was it this, by any chance?" His fingers lingered a moment to tease a tingling nipple. "Or perhaps this is what you had in mind." His fingers continued their feather-light journey to the warm, moist haven between her thighs.

"Any...any of the above will do nicely," she murmured. With a little sigh, she lost herself in the feel of him. "I'll leave the finer points to you."

"I thought you were through with those." Christopher watched Athena climb up on a stool and study a thermistor. She marked something down on her pad, then stepped down.

"Just checking to make sure Angus got the message."

"We gave him his send-off a week ago. You told me he was gone."

"My intuition tells me he has." She took a reading from one of the photocells. "I thought I'd substantiate that a bit more scientifically before I officially close the case." She came down from the stool to find him regarding her seriously—too seriously. She looked up at him brightly, but something inside her turned over.

"And then what, Athena?" he asked her quietly. "What happens after you've closed the case?"

Then I guess all my tomorrows will have finally arrived, she thought. It will be time to pay the price for loving you. "Oh, I don't know," she said aloud, turning away from him to pick up her things. "Perhaps I'll return to North Carolina and get back to work on my doctorate. There are other possibilities. I haven't decided yet."

"I see." She was slipping away from him, but he didn't know how to stop her. The words he silently rehearsed at night when he held her in his arms wouldn't come.

Athena finished putting her things away, hoping he'd go on, praying he would ask her to stay. She longed to tell him she loved him, that leaving would be the hardest thing she'd ever had to do in her life. When he said nothing, she stood and forced herself to smile. "I guess I'd better make up my mind soon. My work here is nearly finished."

"Yes," he said, watching her. "I suppose it is."

Her stomach tightened, and she glanced quickly at her watch. "Oh-oh, I'm late. I promised to take Gram shopping this afternoon." Standing on tiptoe, she gave him a light kiss on his cheek. "We'll be back by teatime. Ask Mary to save us some of her special scones."

The hopelessness hit her on their way back to the castle. While Gram chatted happily about the new dress and hat she had found, Athena was suddenly struck by how much she would miss the old woman, how much she would miss North Berwick. As she followed the winding cliff road, she thought of Christopher. When she had first met him, she'd considered him hard and unbending, rigid, like the rocks below. Now she realized there was far more to him than that. Beneath the scars and hurts of the past, there was a vulnerability few people would ever suspect.

As a child he'd learned to survive by closing himself off, by not acknowledging what hurt him. As an adult, the lesson had been reinforced and Christopher had closed off emotion and love, as well. She knew they couldn't continue on this way. Despite her love for him, she could see no future for them. She needed his love, she had to feel part of him in every possible way. But Christopher wasn't able to share. The one thing he seemed incapable of giving was himself.

The phone call came shortly after she returned home. Athena was still in Gram's room when Christopher called her downstairs.

"It's Peter Scott," he said coolly, handing her the receiver.

She looked searchingly at him, but as soon as she accepted the phone he turned and walked into the library. She waited a moment, then spoke into the receiver.

"Hello, Peter. Yes, I'm fine. And you? Yes, we wrapped it up about a week ago. I'll have to write and tell you all about it. What's going on at the institute?"

Ten minutes later she hung up the phone. Thoughtfully, she turned to see Christopher watching her from the library door.

"When will you be leaving?"

"I haven't agreed to go yet." There was an expectancy in him, a restlessness that hinted at inner turmoil. Yet his eyes remained calm, icy blue shields masking his emotions.

"So he does want you to join him." His words were casual, as if they were discussing tonight's dinner rather than the rest of their lives. "What's his proposition?"

Athena hesitated, then entered the library. She walked over to the fireplace and warmed her hands. "Peter's work in London has attracted the attention of a noted parapsychology periodical. They want him to do an article outlining his research and the findings to date. Since writing isn't one of Peter's strong points, he's asked me to do it for him." He was watching her, his face still expressionless. If she could just get some hint of what he was thinking, some indication of how he felt. "He's agreed to let me include any pertinent information in my doctoral dissertation."

"That's generous of him. Are you going to take him up on it?" He asked the question calmly, but she caught the first faint undertone of emotion in his voice.

"I don't know yet." She turned toward the fire. If he saw her face he'd know. He'd see that she didn't want to leave, that all the articles, all the publicity in the world, weren't as important to her as he was.

"But you're thinking about it."

"Of course I'm thinking about it. It could mean a great deal to my career. Peter's experiments constitute a breakthrough in psychic research."

"And your name on that article would be invaluable, not to mention the use of his findings in your thesis."

Without turning her head from the fire, she nodded.

"You'd be a fool not to accept then."

"Yes, I suppose I would be a fool," she said quietly. "If my career were my major consideration."

"Why shouldn't it be?" he persisted. "Your work is finished here. You have no more commitments to Gram. You're free to leave."

"No one's ever completely free, Christopher." She folded her arms and paced to the window. Dark clouds were gathering overhead, and Athena thought it would probably rain before dinner. She remembered her first night at Burke House. It had stormed then, too. Somehow it all seemed so long ago. She turned back to him. "What do *you* want me to do, Christopher?"

"This is your decision, Athena," he said flatly. "You say this will help your career. You have to do what's best for you."

She searched his face, looking for some sign that he didn't mean it, that he didn't really want her to leave. The shade remained lowered on his feelings, closing her out. But then she'd never really been allowed in, she thought. He had given her his body, but he had never offered to share his soul. Swallowing her pride, she said, "I'm going to miss Burke House. I've grown very fond of Gram—of you."

"You'll be busy," his voice was gruff now, the anger more apparent. "You'll soon forget us."

She felt a surge of frustration. "Just as you'll forget me? Unfortunately I can't turn my emotions on and off as easily as you." She glared at him, furious at him for not caring and at herself for caring too much. She fought back hot tears that stung behind her eyes. "I wish I could turn them off. Life would be so much easier."

"Not always." She heard the pain then, and the loneliness. "Not being able to feel extracts its own pound of flesh."

Athena took a step toward him, then stopped. She longed to reach out and pull him into her arms, but she had tried that and he had not let her in. Megan was wrong, she thought, the hurt a terrible knife in her heart. I'm not the one to bring Christopher back to life after all.

"When you're ready, Lachlan and I will help you bring your things down," he went on emotionlessly.

He turned and walked out, closing the door silently behind him. Athena stood in the middle of the room and wept.

London came to life in May. It bustled with tourists and double-decker buses and bursts of sunshine that turned the gray city to gold. Athena threw herself into the middle of it with a vengeance. She allowed herself no free hours, no time to think. When she wasn't working at Peter's institute, she went sightseeing or rode the Thames or shopped. In the evenings, there were the endless rounds of parties frequented by Peter Scott and his colorful circle of friends.

She found Peter's work fascinating. It was innovative, and in several areas it blazed a bold and adventurous path away from the norm. Athena spent busy days listening and watching, interviewing and taking copious notes. After four weeks she was finally satisfied she had enough information to write the article. When that was completed, she would be ready to return to the States.

At the end of her fifth week in London, Peter astonished her by proposing. "It's a natural," he told her over dinner in one of their favorite Italian restaurants. "We're in the same business, we have basically the same philosophy on life and we're good friends. We should click like a charm."

Athena was having a difficult time not laughing. All through the proposal, Peter had interspersed his words with bites of linguine with clam sauce, and his tone might have been the same had he been suggesting they catch the late movie. She reached across the table and touched his arm. "That's what I like about you, Peter. You're so romantic."

He swallowed a sip of wine and grinned. "Then it's all systems go?"

She shook her head. "It's abort the flight."

He looked interested rather than disappointed. "Why?"

"Because our friendship is too good. Because there's no fire and sparkle between us. And because you're only looking for someone to write your papers for you."

He waved his fork, his mouth full. "Mmm. Another good reason."

She shook her head at him and smiled. "Lastly, because we don't love each other. Not that way."

"We could learn."

"We could also fall flat on our faces."

Peter wiped his mouth with his napkin and studied her too astutely. "You're still in love with Burke, aren't you?"

Athena looked at him in surprise. She hadn't mentioned Christopher once since coming to London. "What makes you think that?"

"Unfortunately, you've got all the symptoms. You keep yourself busy—too busy—running here, there and everywhere, never stopping. You don't eat unless I sit you down and put the food in front of you. And every so often you get a wistful expression on your face like a lovesick calf."

She burst out laughing. "Do I really? I'll have to remember that."

He used the last of his French bread to soak up clam sauce. "So what are you going to do about it?"

"I've already done everything I could—without using my pride as a doormat." She felt her stomach muscles tighten. She didn't want to talk about it.

"Come on," he prodded. "I'm the doctor, remember. You've got to face it sooner or later."

"I was opting for later." She looked at him over her wine, then shook her head. "You're not going to let me squirm out of this, are you?"

"No way. If he asked, would you go back to him?"

"I don't know," she answered helplessly. "Even if he asked me back, I just can't see a future for us. He closed himself off from me. My loving him isn't enough. I'd have to know that he returned that love."

"And so you'll wait."

"What?"

"You'll wait until he can love you back."

She shook her head. "I have no intentions of waiting. As soon as my work here is finished, I plan to go home."

He shrugged. "You may go home, and you may exorcise a few ghosts and you'll probably knock everyone on their ears with your doctoral thesis. But you won't forget him." He gave her a cheerful wink. "I know you pretty well by now, Athena. One of your best and your worst qualities is that you're so damn stubborn. You just don't like to give up. No matter what's going on with you on the outside, inside you'll still be waiting for him."

Athena laughed. But long after they had parted for the night, she wondered if Peter could be right.

By the third week in June she had finished the article. It had been accepted, and she'd soon been assured the check was in the mail. She had six notebooks brimming with information about Peter's experiments—much more than she would ever need for her dissertation. Athena could no longer postpone the inevitable. It was time to go home.

If Christopher was going to come, he would have arrived long before this, she told herself for the thousandth time. By now he had probably forgotten her. He was undoubtedly up to his ears in new buildings and shopping malls and whatever else occupied a successful entrepreneur. At least Gram continued to do well. They'd already exchanged several letters, and Athena was relieved that there'd been no further sign of Angus MacKay.

She had also heard from Christopher's solicitors concerning Kildrurry. The change in title was being duly processed, and she could expect to hear from them shortly. Everything was being taken care of. There was nothing left to hold her in London.

Except her unflagging hope. Peter had been right. She was painfully slow to give up. Although she realized she'd been dragging her heels about leaving, she continued to give it just one more day—one more chance to find him standing at her door.

By the end of June, however, even Athena was ready to give up hope. She made her airline reservations, telegraphed her mother when she was arriving and prepared to enjoy her last night in London. She'd already declined one of Peter's party invitations, preferring to say her own quiet goodbye to England. For the first time in two months, she wanted to be alone.

She had just rinsed the shampoo out of her hair when she heard the doorbell. By the third ring, she had grabbed a towel and was padding over to answer it. Tucking the towel between her breasts, she reached for the door. "Peter, if you're here to try to talk me into going to that—"

She looked up at him and froze. Christopher watched the color drain out of her face and saw her clench the doorjamb for support.

"Hello, Athena."

The sound of his voice snapped her out of her shock. "Christopher. I didn't expect to see you."

"No. Actually, I made the decision to come to Londo rather suddenly. While I was in town I thought I'd drop of the deed to Kildrurry."

"Oh." She felt a letdown so painful she nearly cried out He hadn't come for her at all. He'd come to deliver th deed. Suddenly Athena wished she'd never heard of th damn keep! "Won't you come in? I just . . . I just got ou of the shower. If you'll wait a minute I'll throw on som clothes."

"If you're going out, I won't stay." He tried to keep h eyes off her. Every line of her body seemed to shout out a him from beneath the towel. "I should have called first."

"No, it's all right, really. I'm not going out—at least was, but just by myself. There's no hurry." She closed th door behind him, then stood there clutching her towe feeling awkward and incredibly tongue-tied. "I'll, ah, ju be a minute. Sit down and make yourself comfortable."

He was too restless to sit. Instead he paced to the wir dow and looked down at the street. He avoided Londo He usually avoided all the places where Ryan and Sylv had lived. He knew it was irrational to think he might ru into them in a city this size. But Christopher knew h wasn't always rational when it came to his brother and e wife.

He let the curtain fall and examined the room. It was furnished apartment, but with a touch here and ther Athena had stamped her mark on the room. It held su shine and laughter—all the things that had been missir from his life since she'd left Scotland. She had taken th magic with her, leaving behind an emptiness he had no been able to fill.

When she came back into the room, he looked at he more closely. She had put on slacks and a blouse, but h feet were still bare. She looked thinner then he remembered, too thin. But she was breathtakingly lovely. He had forgotten nothing about her—the way her chestnut curls scattered about her head, the way her eyes changed from brown to gold to green, the direct way she had of looking at you as if you were the most fascinating person in the room. *How have I lived two months without her?* he thought.

"London agrees with you, Athena."

"Thank you." She could hardly look at him. Every time she did she felt the pain like a knife in her heart. *How am I going to get through this without making a fool of myself?* she wondered. "Would you care for a drink?" She hurried into the kitchen. "I can offer you Chablis and, ah, Chablis. Sorry, my stock is low."

"That will be fine." He moved into the tiny kitchen and watched her pour wine into two water glasses. *She doesn't entertain much,* he thought. And he could see no signs of Scott hanging about the place.

"Are you in town long?" she asked, handing him a glass.

"That depends on how my business goes." He reached into his pocket. "Before I forget, here's the deed."

She held it in her hand, marveling that so much had happened because of one piece of paper. "How's Gram?"

"She's fine." He hesitated. "She misses you."

"I miss her, too." She stared at him awkwardly, then moved to the couch and sat down. Idly she scanned the deed, then read the date of transfer twice. "Christopher, this isn't right. This document is dated almost two weeks before I left Burke House. It was the day you went to Brussels."

"That's when I signed it over to you. Before I left Scotland, I saw my solicitors."

"But that was the day before I found the copy in the records office—before we found Angus."

"I tried to tell you there was no need to prove you claim."

Her eyes widened. "But why?"

"Because I saw how much Kildrurry meant to you. Because after our weekend in Edinburgh I knew I could neve tear it down for a golf course."

"You must have lost a great deal of money."

"Dammit, Athena. Despite what you think of me, I d value some things more than money."

She stared at the deed for a long moment. "Thank you Christopher. It means even more to me this way." Sh stood and walked to the window. "Gram wrote me. Sh said that Burke Enterprises was establishing a fund to re store Kildrurry. That's very generous of you."

"It's little enough under the circumstances."

"Yes, well, thank you anyway." She turned to look o the window. Every minute he stayed here was making that much more difficult for her to let him go again. Sh took a deep breath and tried to keep the conversation ligh "Gram says there have been no more signs of Angus."

"No. It's been very quiet." Too quiet, he thought. Sin she'd left it was as if Burke House had become a mauso leum. His hands gripped the back of a chair. "Athena, want you to come back to Scotland with me."

She didn't move. Her heart seemed suspended in time she continued to stare out the window. "Would . . . wou you please repeat that?"

"I said I want you to come home with me." He mov from the chair but kept his hands clenched tightly at h

es to keep from touching her. He was afraid he might
e her if he did. His possessive fear had driven her away
the first place. He could not afford to make the same
stake again.

Athena turned away from the window to face him.
Come?" She repeated the word as if she were testing its
aning. "You mean Burke House?"

"Yes."

"Why?" She was watching his eyes. She would know,
told herself, if she watched his eyes. "Why do you
nt me to come back?"

Now that the time had come, he didn't know how to tell
. Where were the words to explain something he still
n't fully understand himself? "I love you, Athena," he
d quietly. "I want you to come back because the house
mpty—*I'm* empty—without you."

He hesitated. His mind was racing, crowded with
rything he wanted to tell her, unsure of how to begin.
efore I met you I thought I didn't need anyone any-
re. I'd closed myself off for so long I'd forgotten what
vas like to feel and to care. Toward the end I even closed
am off. I watched her get older and I was afraid of what
uld happen when I lost her."

He stopped again, but his eyes never left her face. "I
ught love was for dreamers. I resented the way you
de me lose control because it forced me to feel, and
ling was the one thing I had vowed never to do again. I
l myself that what I felt toward you was purely physi-
, that when you left everything would be the way it was
ore. But it isn't the same. Nothing in my life will ever
the same again."

She was watching him, and she read the truth on [
face. He'd said he loved her. The words echoed inside l
head. He loved her, but could he share himself with he

"You told me to go, Christopher. You told me to go
London."

"I thought that's what you wanted. I was afraid tha
I asked you to stay, sooner or later you'd grow restless a
leave. I was confused. Things were happening to me an
wasn't sure I wanted them to. I was changing and you w
responsible."

"We all change, Christopher. None of us ever stay
same. We grow through love and we grow through pa
And we change."

"But I didn't want to change. I was afraid to feel aga
to love. When I found myself caring too much for yo
searched for your faults. I tried to tell myself you wer
fraud, a schemer. I wanted to believe you would do a
thing to get Kildrurry."

She still hadn't moved from the window, and behind
he saw the dusk of the day turn to night. He studied
face as he went on. "The weekend we spent in Edinbu
I realized that despite all my efforts I was falling in l
with you. The night you had dinner with Scott I had j
finished signing Kildrurry over. I felt betrayed. I told
self you were no better than Sylvia, willing to use me ;
then run off at the first promising opportunity. Since
never worked out my anger and hurt toward her, I
leashed it all on you—ten years of bottled up rese
ment."

He looked at her, but he couldn't tell if she underst
what he was trying to say. "When Scott called that
night, I decided it was better to cut the tie then and the
before I became even more entangled. I was becoming

dependent on you. You'd brought laughter, sunshine into my life, but you had the power to take it all away just as quickly. And because you had taught me how to feel again, I was afraid."

Athena had a difficult time imagining Christopher being afraid of anything, especially her. How little she really knew of him, she thought, sensing his pain. How much she was learning.

"Your work at Burke House was finished," he went on. "I didn't know how to keep you there—I didn't know if I *wanted* to keep you there. I was afraid of loving you and I was afraid of losing you. The suspense of watching you day after day wondering when you were going to pack up and say goodbye was terrible."

"All you had to do was ask me to stay," she said quietly.

"Did I, Athena?" He started toward her, then stopped. The urge to hold her in his arms was nearly overpowering. "Perhaps I wasn't ready to ask you then. I still thought I could make it alone, the same way I had before you came into my life." He thought of the endless weeks he had spent without her, the days and nights that seemed more like years. "But you'd taken the light and the laughter with you, and I found I didn't want to live in the darkness once more. You'd taught me how to feel and I'd lost the ability to close myself off again. For the first time in years I needed someone. I needed you."

Athena felt as if her heart was going to burst. He loved her—he needed her. How many nights had she lain awake imagining him saying those words! "Oh, Christopher," she cried. "You great fool! Didn't it ever occur to you that I might need you, too?"

Before he had taken two steps toward her, she had flown across the room and into his arms. "How I've missed you!" She found his mouth and effectively blocked any more words. "Hold me tight. That's what I've missed most. Just hold me."

"I never thought I'd hear you say that again." He pulled her against him, knowing that this time he would not have to let her go. "Athena, I love you so much."

"Please. Say it again."

"If you'll let me, I'll say it to you every day for the rest of our lives." Holding her shoulders, he drew her away until he could look into her face. "Athena, will you marry me?"

She laughed, feeling dizzy and crazy and amazingly clearheaded all at the same time. "Will you give me time to put on my shoes?"

"Only if you insist. I'd take you without a stitch on your back."

She looked up at him, her face beaming. "That can be arranged."

He swept her back into his arms and gave her a long frenzied kiss, trying to pack two months of loneliness into one embrace. "How have I managed without you?" he murmured. His lips couldn't get enough of her. They flew across her face, her hair, her neck, trying to taste everything at once. "I love you, Athena. More than anything in the world, I love you."

She buried her face in his chest, and this time she did nothing to stop the tears that flooded her eyes. She felt as if she were going to burst with joy. Two months ago she'd prayed for a miracle. Now it was here in her arms.

He tilted her face with his finger. "Hey, why the tears?"

Athena looked into his eyes. They were brimming with emotion—love, happiness, excitement, tenderness. He was feeling. The shield was down. He was letting her in!

"Because you're willing to love and to care again. Because you're sharing it with me." She reached up for his lips. "And because I've never been happier in my life!"

OFFICIAL SWEEPSTAKES INFORMATION

1. **NO PURCHASE NECESSARY.** To enter, complete the official entry/order form. Be sure to indicate whether or not you wish to take advantage of our subscription offer.

2. Entry blanks have been pre-selected for the prizes offered. Your response will be checked to see if you are a winner. In the event that these are not claimed, a random drawing will be held from all entries received to award not less than $150,000 in prizes. This is in addition to any free, surprise or mystery gifts which might be offered. Versions of this sweepstakes with different prizes will appear in Torstar Ltd. mailings and their affiliates. Winners selected will receive the prize offered in their sweepstakes insert.

3. This promotion is being conducted under the supervision of Marden-Kane, an independent judging organization. By entering the sweepstakes, each entrant accepts and agrees to be bound by these rules and the decisions of the judges which shall be final and binding. Odds of winning in the random drawing are dependent upon the total number of entries received. Taxes, if any, are the sole responsibility of the prize winners. Prizes are non-transferable. All entries must be received by August 31, 1986.

4. This sweepstakes package offers:

1, Grand Prize	:	Cruise around the world on the QEII	$100,000 total value
4, First Prizes	:	Set of matching pearl necklace and earrings	$ 20,000 total value
10, Second Prizes:		Romantic Weekend in Bermuda	$ 15,000 total value
25, Third Prizes	:	Designer Luggage	$ 10,000 total value
200, Fourth Prizes :		$25 Gift Certificate	$ 5,000 total value
			$150,000

Winners may elect to receive the cash equivalent for the prizes offered.

5. This offer is open to residents of the U.S. and Canada, 18 years and older, except employees of Torstar Ltd., its affiliates, subsidiaries, Marden-Kane and all other agencies and persons connected with conducting this sweepstakes. All Federal, State and local laws apply. Void in the province of Quebec and wherever prohibited or restricted by law. Winners will be notified by mail and may be required to execute an affidavit of eligibility and release which must be returned within 14 days after notification. Canadian winners will be required to answer a skill testing question. Winners consent to the use of their names, photograph and/or likeness for advertising and publicity purposes in conjunction with this and similar promotions without additional compensation. One prize per family or household.

6. For a list of our most current prize winners, send a stamped, self-addressed envelope to: WINNERS LIST, c/o Marden-Kane, P.O. Box 10404, Long Island City, New York 11101.